KERORO GUNSOU

VOL #12

BY MINE YOSHIZAKI

RORO 2006

KERORO PIN-UP

SERGEANT-K

SGT. FROG 12 • TABLE OF CONTENTS

VOLUME #12

BY
MINE YOSHIZAKI

AMBURG // LONDON // LOS ANGELES // TOKYO

Sgt. Frog Vol. 12

Created By Mine Yoshizaki

Translation - Yuko Fukami
Associate Editor - Peter Ahlstrom
Retouch and Lettering - Courtney Geter
Cover Design - James Lee

Editor - Paul Morrissey
Digital Imaging Manager - Chris Buford
Pre-Production Supervisor - Erika Terriquez
Art Director - Anne Marie Horne
Production Manager - Elisabeth Brizzi
Managing Editor - Vy Nguyen
VP of Production - Ron Klamert
Editor-in-Chief - Rob Tokar
Publisher - Mike Kiley
President and C.O.O. - John Parker
C.E.O. and Chief Creative Officer - Stuart Levy

A  Manga

TOKYOPOP Inc.
5900 Wilshire Blvd. Suite 2000
Los Angeles, CA 90036

E-mail: info@TOKYOPOP.com
Come visit us online at www.TOKYOPOP.com

ISBN: 1-59816-865-7

First TOKYOPOP printing: December 2006

10 9 8 7 6 5 4 3 2 1

Printed in the USA

CHARACTER RELATIONSHIPS AND THE STORY SO FAR

(FACT-CHECKING PERFORMED BY SHONEN ACE MAGAZINE)

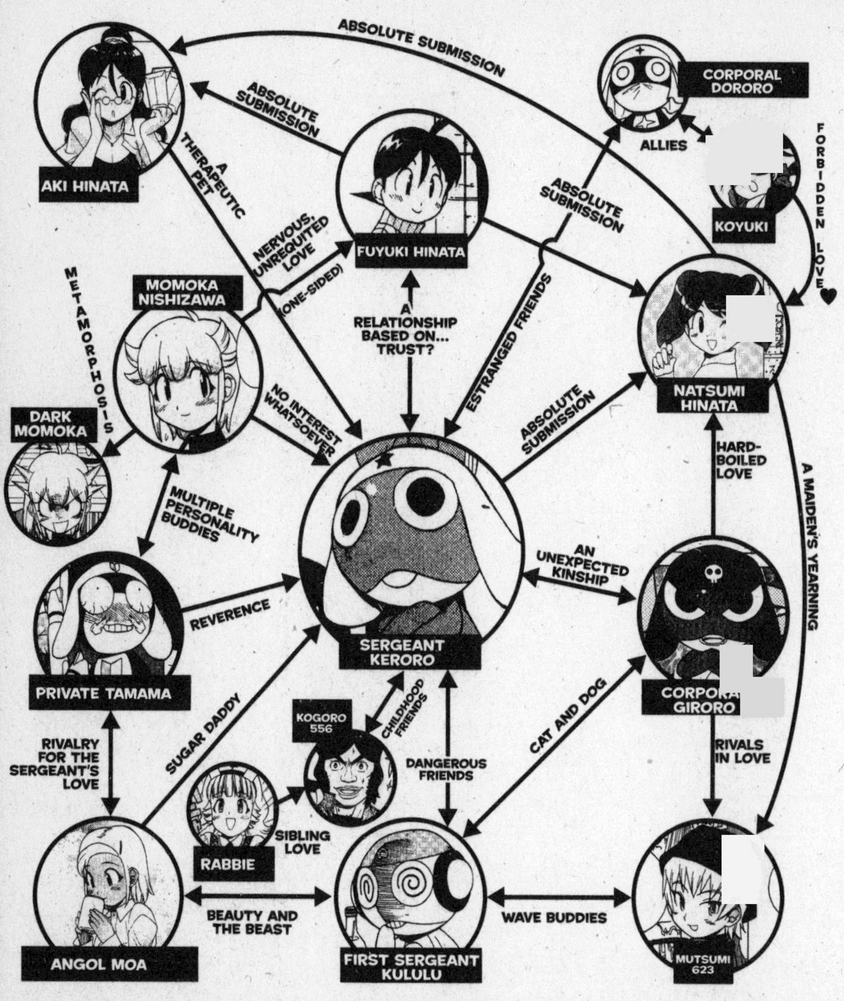

AS CAPTAIN OF THE SPACE INVASION FORCE'S SPECIAL ADVANCE TEAM OF THE 58TH PLANET OF THE GAMMA STORM CLOUD SYSTEM, SGT. KERORO ENTERED THE HINATA FAMILY WHEN HIS PRE-ATTACK PREPARATION FOR THE INVASION OF EARTH RAN AFOUL VIA HIS EASY CAPTURE BY THE HINATA CHILDREN, FUYUKI AND NATSUMI. THANKS TO FUYUKI'S KINDNESS, OR RATHER HIS CURIOSITY, SGT. KERORO SOON BECAME A WARD OF THE HINATA HOME, WITH FREE ROOM AND BOARD IN EXCHANGE FOR HOUSEWORK. BUT EVEN AS HE SCRUBBED THE HINATAS' DISHES, KERORO WAS CROUCHED LIKE THE PROVERBIAL TIGER, READY TO SPRING THE ULTIMATE INVASION ON POKOPEN...AS SOON AS HE FINISHED COLLECTING GUNDAM MODELS, UPDATING HIS WEBPAGE AND DEVELOPING AN APPRECIATION FOR THE FINER POINTS OF JAPANESE CULTURE! RECENTLY, KERORO WAS FORCED TO FACE OFF AGAINST THE FORMIDABLE GARURU PLATOON--SENT BY THE KERON FORCE TO COLLECT ITS WAYWARD SERGEANT AND FINALLY DESTROY EARTH, ONCE AND FOR ALL. BUT THE DAY WAS SAVED, AS IT ALWAYS IS...AND KERORO AND FRIENDS WERE ONCE AGAIN LEFT TO THEIR OWN USELESS DEVICES! HURRAH!

Hup! Two, three, four!

Two! Two, three, four!

ENCOUNTER XCII
STRICTLY FORBIDDEN: A HARD-BOILED BAN!

HARD-BOILED
A LIFESTYLE DICTATED BY DUTY, RATHER THAN EMOTION.
HRMM ...
squeek squeek
GIRORO

HE COLDLY POLISHES THE WEAPONS ...
Kyu kyu...
はぁぁ
...RUTH-LESSLY TAGS THE WEAPONS CAT ALOGUE ...
Mua ha ha.
...AND UNFEEL-INGLY STOKES THE FIRE.
pop crackle
pop
GRR
ZZZ

HE IS THE RED DHARMA... NO. THE DEVIL OF THE BATTLEFIELD. HE IS THE HARD-BOILED ONE. THE ONE KNOWN ONLY AS--
GIRORO!!
N-NATSUMI?!
!
KABOOM

HAH... HUMPH! WHAT DO YOU WANT?
DON'T STAND BEHIND ME LIKE THAT...
squeak squeak
wipe wipe
WHA?!!
drip
drip
fizzle fizzle

A BONFIRE?! ON A HOT DAY LIKE **THIS**?!
YOUR STUPID FIRE MADE MY LAUNDRY ALL SMOKY!!
WHA WHA WHAAA ?!

I HEREBY **FORBID** FIRES!!
THEY'RE BANNED! GOT IT, BUSTER?!!

NA--
NA-TSUMI ...?
click click
UMP GRUMP GRUMP GRUMP

GRUMP
GRUM
WHAT IS THIS HEAVY FEELING...?
UH-OH ... THIS CAN'T BE GOOD!
GRUMP
GRUMP GRUMP GRUMP GRUM

SER-GEANT-- C'MERE!
bip
bip
G-gero?
SNEAK...

WHAT'S GOING ON WITH MASTER NATSUMI ?!
EEEEEE...
Phew!
DUNNO, BUT I THINK SHE'S IN A BAD MOOD!

BE VERY CAREFUL, SER-GEANT!
WHEN NATSUMI'S IN A BAD MOOD...

...SHE TENDS TO... FORBID THINGS.
forbid
TO A POINT THAT'S NOT JUST ABSURD...BUT DOWNRIGHT SCARY!!!
Occult is for-bidden!!
B-but-- how can you ban my very existence --?
You want me to show ya?!

I'M GOING TO STAY IN MY ROOM AND RIDE THIS THING OUT.
WHATEVER YOU DO, SERGEANT-- JUST--STAY AWAY FROM NATSUMI!!
hide hide
...HOW VERY VEXING.

Oh ho ho!
WELL, BETTER TAKE THESE... CAN'T LET NATSUMI'S TEMPER INTERFERE WITH MY GUNDAM-BUILDING!
ESPECIALLY NOT MY PRECIOUS HGUC GUN CANNON!
YEEEP?!
WHOSE TEMPER?!!
WELL, NO, I'M--YOU'RE JUST SO-- WHOA!
JUST SO...?
G-G-GUNDAM MODELS KNOW NO CRIME!!
WHEN I WORK ON A GUNDAM MODEL, I AM HARMLESS, LIKE THE PIGEON!!
IT IS A PIGEON, ISN'T IT? YES! THE VERY SYMBOL OF PEACE!
jumble mumble mumble
Mumble
LET'S THINK THIS THROUGH RATIONALLY, MASTER NATSUMI!
SURELY THERE MUST BE SOMETHING ELSE YOU CAN FORBID!!
OH? LIKE WHAT?
wheeze
wheeze
EEP!
SOME-THING... ELSE... WELL... YES...! UH... HUH...
IF YOU'RE JUST GOING TO BLATHER... THEN I FORBID--
GERO-WAHH! JUST ONE MOMENT!!
WAIT!
WAIT!
YES...
PERFECT!!

DAZE

A SOLDIER KEEPS HIS MIND JUST AS HE KEEPS HIS FORTRESS...
STRONG AND STABLE, LIKE A MOUNTAIN...
THE WAY NATSUMI WAS JUST NOW...
SHE HATES ME... SHE HATES ME...
ARRGH! WHAT AM I DOING?!
THINKING?? AT A TIME LIKE THIS?!

A MAN DOESN'T THINK—HE POLISHES HIS GUN!
TIME TO SHARPEN THE SOUL OF THE SOLDIER!!
OKURE
565
キンゾクミ
Economy size!
Wet-Tish
YES... THAT'S MORE LIKE IT!
TO BE AFFECTED BY SUCH A TRIVIAL THING...I'VE GONE SOFT, IT SEEMS...

YOU!!!
GYAAAAAH!!
......?
Violation!
Violation!
NA... NATSUMI ?!!
NO...IT CAN'T BE...
WHAT IS THIS?!
I am ordinance patrol machine No.723.
Burp
My orders are to seek out ordinance violators.
O-ORDI-NANCE ...?!
This area has been designated: Weapons Free.
WHA... WHAT ?!
NO WEAPONS
BAM!

F-FOOLISH! WHO WOULD DO SUCH AN IDIOTIC THING?! AND WHEN ?!
WHAT? N-NA-TSUMI ?!
Natsumi Hinata designated this area a Weapons Free Zone today.
There are a number of approved penalties for violators.
For the safety and comfort of others, your cooperation is appreciated.
Penetrates up to 723 layers of metal.
Blizzard Natsu At -723 degrees, it feels hot rather than cold.
Summer Fire Flame of 723 degrees. A positive number with vivid heat.
BUT I WAS JUST POLISHING!!!
A weapon is a weapon.
NO...I CAN'T ALLOW THIS!!
NORMALLY, I WOULD SHOOT THIS THING DOWN IN A FLASH!
BUT THE WAY IT'S DESIGNED...
ARGHH! IT'S NOT FAIR!!

ALL RIGHT. FINE!
I'LL LEAVE THIS AREA. ARE YOU SATISFIED ?!
Violation.
C-C-C-COLD!!!

For a pleasant environment...
...please, mind your manners.

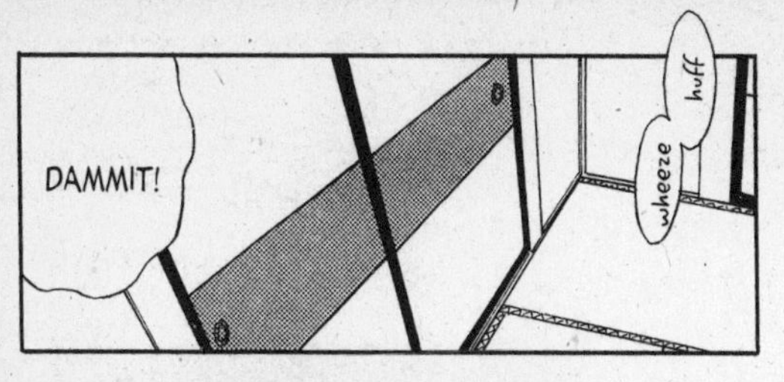
huff
wheeze
DAMMIT!

WELL! IT'LL NEVER FIND ME IN HERE.
WHAT A MAN WILL GO THROUGH TO GET SOME PEACE...

NOW...
Heh...
SQUIK
KA-BOOM!
NO WEAPONS
?!!

Violation.
HOT!! HOT, HOT, HOT!!!

DAMMIT... I WILL CLEAN THIS WEAPON...
...IF IT KILLS ME!

EEEK!
Violation.
NOOOOOOOOO!
GYAAAAH!
Polishing weapons may be harmful to your health.
GYAAAAAH!
And may pose a danger to the public as well.
Gero Gero Gero Gero!
SO I SAYS TO MASTER NATSUMI--I SAYS-- "WHY DON'T YOU BAN ALL WEAPONS?"
IT AIN'T LIKE WE USE THEM ANYWAY! ♪
AH HA HAHA HA!
munch
crunch
THAT WAS A WONDERFUL IDEA! ♡

OF COURSE... IF SWEETS WERE FORBIDDEN ...
...OR IF GUNDAM MODELS WERE FORBIDDEN ...
COULDN'T LET THAT HAPPEN!
Gero! Gero Gero Gero!
Gero?!
GI... GIRORO?!
SO THAT'S IT!
THE SOUL OF OUR PLATOON, OUR SOUL...
YOU TWO... YOU WOULD DARE...!
S-SOUL ...?
B-BUT-- WE HAVEN'T DONE ANYTHING!
KA-BAM!
YOU CALL YOURSELVES SOLDIERS!!
CORPORAL GIRORO CAN ACCESS ANY OF HIS WEAPONS ANYTIME, VIA DIMENSIONAL TRANSFER!
GEROOO ?!!

C-CALM DOWN, GIRORO, SIR.
Y-YES! PLEASE!
YOU CALL YOURSELVES SOLDIERS!!
ACK! HE'S REPEATING HIMSELF!
NOW WE'RE REALLY IN FOR IT!
S-SEE?! THIS IS A FORBIDDEN AREA!
I'M SAYING THIS FOR YOU!!
Violation.
HM! YES! CAN'T BE HELPED!
IT WAS HIM! THAT GUY OVER THERE! HE'S GOT THE WEAPON!
See?
There!
?!
FOOOOO ?!!
WHYYYYY MEEEEE?!
THUD

The instrument in your hand is designed to scrape objects. Therefore, it has the potential to destroy.
It can be used as a weapon.
And this one's entire body is a weapon. His existence itself is a violation.
crik crik crik

We all must observe the ordinances.
The only alternative is death.

AHH... ANOTHER OF MY CREATIONS EVOLVES.
Ku ku ku ku...
THOUGH, OF COURSE, I PROG-RAMMED IT THAT WAY...
Ku ku ku ku
......!
HUH?!
beep beep
Violation detected.
Weapon in the kitchen.
KITCHEN...?
NO... COULD IT BE ...?!

NOW, WHY WAS I FEELING SO GROUCHY EARLIER?
I GUESS I SHOULD LEARN TO CONTROL MY TEMPER...
SLICE
SLICE
I REALLY SHOULDN'T HAVE TAKEN IT OUT ON GIRORO.
MAYBE HE'LL ACCEPT THESE AS A PEACE OFFERING...?
SLICE
Violation. Violation.
BEEP
This area has been designated: Weapons Free...
SHIVER
...?!
...by Natsumi Hinata.
WHAT? ME? NO!
WAIT A MINUTE... WHAT DID THAT STUPID FROG SAY EARLIER...?
NATSUMIII!
?!

Violation.
Violatio --?
YOU ARE...
...IN VIOLATION!!
That... is... correct!
beep
beep
beep
beep
beep
I... have the weapon... I am in violation...
TMP
BOOM
I'LL SEE YOU... AND YOUR STUPID ORDINANCE... IN HELL.
......

TH- THANKS, GIRORO.
HUMPH! AS LONG AS YOU'RE OKAY, IT'S FINE.
UMM... GIRORO...
BADUM!
I'M SOR--
STOP!

IT'S NOT BECOMING OF YOU.
I FORBID YOU TO APOLOGIZE!

EVEN IF IT MAKES US RED WITH EMBARRASSMENT TO WATCH...
......
Whoa...
A MAN OF PRINCIPLE... THAT'S OUR HARD-BOILED CORPORAL GIRORO!
ER... KERORO-KUN? WHEN DO I GET TO APPEAR?
DON'T TELL ME I'M FORBIDDEN TO MAKE AN AP-PEARANCE!
TO BE CONTINUED

WHOA!
お ーっ
CITIZENS OF POKOPEN: DO YOU LIKE BATHS?
IT SEEMS THAT BATHS ARE SPECIAL FOR ALIENS, TOO...

WOW! INCREDIBLE!
I'M SO IMPRESSED!
SEE? SEE?
ENCOUNTER XCIII
SPLENDOR IN THE TUB

WELL! I'M GOING TO ENJOY THIS RIGHT AWAY!
THANKS FOR THE HARD WORK!
GERO. HAVE A NICE, RELAXING TIME.
WOO HOO! I RULE!
splish
splash
shaaaaa...
MASTER NATSUMI SEEMS QUITE PLEASED!
GUESS I'LL GO TAKE A BATH MYSELF, BACK AT THE BASE.
......

BUT WAIT!!!
I'VE NEVER ONCE ALLOWED MYSELF...
Humm humm
SPLISH
SPLISH
...TO ENJOY A PRISTINE, SPARKLING BATHTUB THAT I MYSELF SCRUBBED AND CLEANED!
SCREEE
A VERY IMPORTANT TRUTH HAS SUDDENLY DAWNED ON ME!
I HAVE ALWAYS YIELDED THE "RIGHT OF SPARKLING BATH" TO POKOPENIANS... AS IF IT WERE THEIR GOD-GIVEN RIGHT!
Ahhhh...

FARMERS WERE UNABLE TO EAT THE RICE THEY GREW...(ANCIENT HISTORY)
THE TAXES WE PAY ARE WASTED ON USELESS PUBLIC PROJECTS... (SAW ON TV YESTERDAY)
WHAT A TWISTED CUSTOM... SUCH INJUSTICE IS UNIQUE TO POKOPEN!!
WE MUST INVADE THIS PLANET IMMEDIATELY!!

SNEAK...
SPLASH
SPLASH

WELL, NOTHING A LITTLE SCHVITZ WON'T CURE!
OH, MASTER NATSUUUMIII! I'M COMING IN TO JOIIIN YOUUU! ♡

...YOU MEAN, TOGETHER?
...LIKE, YOU AND ME?
UH-HUH!
SURE!
KARA KARA KARA
IN YOUR DREAMS, YOU NASTY FROG!!!
SUCH... INJUSTICE..
SLAM!
INJUSTICE MY BUTT!
INJUSTICE...
SOMETHING COMPLETELY UNFAIR OR UNJUSTIFIED.
FOR EXAMPLE: GETTING MUD SPLASHED ALL OVER YOU WHILE WALKING DOWN THE STREET.
TOTALLY UNJUST!
WANTED

SERGEANT!
THE ONE WHO MADE THE BATH SPARKLE IS THE ONE WHO GETS ALL MUDDY?!
TO TALLY UN-JUST!!
MASTER FUYUKI!
LOOK AT YOUR FACE!!
AH HA HA HA!
SPEAK FOR YOURSELF, MASTER FUYUKI! YOU LOOK DOWNRIGHT AWFUL!!
WELL, I'D BETTER WASH THIS OFF...
HEY!
SERGEANT! I HAVE AN IDEA!
LET'S TAKE A BATH TOGETHER!
Gero?!
WANTED
I DON'T THINK WE'VE EVER TAKEN A BATH TOGETHER!
IT'LL BE FUN! WE CAN WASH EACH OTHER OFF!
Gerooo! AYE-AYE, SIR!
PHEW... THAT WAS NICE! ♪
NOTHING LIKE A NICE, HOT BATH.
YAHOOOOO!!

どど
I'M FIRST!
FUYUKI ?!
どど!!
NO WAY! I'M FIRST!!
WHAT THE...?
SHOOOM
WAAAAAH!
SINCE POKOPENIANS HAVE ALL THAT EXTRA JUNK ON THEIR BODIES, I'LL GO FIRST!
HEY-- WAIT A MINUTE!
SHOOOP
ぴょーん!
HERE I GO! FIRST IN THE TUB!!
がし
じゃばー
WHAAAAA?!
YOU HAVE TO WASH OFF THE MUD FIRST!
Ge...ro...

KER-SPLASH!

AHHHHH ... ♪
KER-SPLISH!
THIS IS HEAVEN... ♪

SERGEANT... DO ALIENS LIKE BATHS, TOO?
NATURALLY!!!

THEY'RE WET THEY'RE WARM. THEY REFRESH THE BODY AND SOUL!
BATHS HELP GET US THROUGH ALL OF OUR GRUELING INVASION SCHEMES!
WELL... MAYBE THAT'S NOT SO GOOD... BUT...

MASTER FUYUKI, LET'S SEE WHO CAN STAY UNDER-WATER THE LONGEST! THE PRIZE IS POKOPEN!
WELL, OKAY! I WON'T BET THE EARTH ON IT, THOUGH.

GO!!

I WON'T LOSE TO THE SERGEANT!

AH HA HA HA HA!
HEY--NO FAIR, SERGEANT!!

Gero Gero Gero! I'VE DEFEATED MANY ENEMIES WITH THAT TRICK!
ALL RIGHT... I GIVE UP.
AND NOW! ANOTHER OF MY 48 FAMOUS BATH TRICKS!
A JUMPING SEQUENCE, USING THE SURFACE TENSION OF WATER!!
ぱしゃ
ぱしゃー

WOW! IT'S LOTS OF FUN TAKING A BATH WITH YOU, SERGEANT!
THE BATHTUB IS THE ONLY PLACE WHERE YOU CAN SHOW YOUR TRUE SELF!
IT'S TRUE. KERONIANS USE BATHS TO DEEPEN THEIR FRIENDSHIPS.
I WILL SHOW YOU A SPECIAL FRIENDSHIP RITUAL OF KERON.
REALLY? SHOW ME! SHOW ME!

TO BE CONTINUED

G-GROUND-BREAKING!!
IT'S GOOD... YES! THIS IS GOING TO WORK!!
AGGRESSION PLAN-X

KU KU KU KU... SUCCESS RATE: 180 PERCENT! IT'LL SUCCEED EVEN IF YOU'RE HALF ASLEEP.
THIS KINDA THING DON'T COME 'ROUND EVERY DAY. IT'S BITCHIN', MAN!

FINALLY... FINALLY...THE DAY WE INVADE POKOPEN IS HERE!!
WE'RE THE BRIGHTEST BUNCH IN THE COSMOS AFTER ALL!!
Call me when you're done.

WE'VE ALL EXPERIENCED IT...THE WONDER OF INSPIRATION. A MIRACULOUS FLASH...A BOLT FROM THE BLUE...
MISTER SERGEANT!
KERORO!!
CAPTAIN ...
AND AT THAT VERY MOMENT, OUR HONORABLE SERGEANT...
ENCOUNTER XCIV KERORO FALLS ILL; CHAOS ENSUES!

HUH?
OH, YES?
AH!
WHAT? SORRY...I WASN'T LISTENING!

...IS CLEARLY SHOWING SIGNS OF ABNOR-MALITY!
I SEE. SO! ABOUT TIME FOR AN INVASION, EH...?
shiver shiver
HMM. THIS SOUNDS PRETTY GOOD. LET'S DO IT. LET'S DO IT.
UH, KERORO...
Call me when you're done.

SERGEANT... IS SOME-THING WRONG?
WHO? ME?

NONSENSE! I'M THE SAME AS ALWAYS...
shake
shake shake

WHY, I CAN JUST SEE THOSE POKOPENIANS PANICKING RIGHT NOW.
DON'T WORRY... EVERY-THING'S GOING TO BE JUST...
PSHHHT

ENCOUNTER XCIV
KERORO FALLS ILL; CHAOS ENSUES!
MORE

CLINK
CLINK
CLINK
SQUIK
SQUIK
SQUIK
SQUIK
SQUIK
SQUIK
SQUIK
UH...
HOW LONG ARE YOU GOING TO DRY THAT SAME GLASS?
EH?
SQUIK

SHAKE
!!
WATCH IT!!
GAH! WHAT DO YOU THINK YOU'RE DOING, STUPID FROG?!
I'M... SORRY.
? ...

LOOK, I'LL DO THE REST-- COULD YOU JUST GO GET THE BATH READY?
AYE-AYE, SIR.
THE STUPID FROG...
...HAS HE ALWAYS BEEN THAT LIGHT?
I'M HOOOME!
SORRY, SERGEANT. I COULDN'T FIND THAT GUNDAM MODEL YOU WANTED.
THAT ONE CALLED AGGAI, IN THE BIG BOX, RIGHT?
IT WAS ALL SOLD OUT.
TMP TMP TMP
UGH, SOME-ONE LEFT THE HOT WATER ON.
WHAT WERE THEY THINKING?
!?

SERGEANT ?!!
FLOAT
FLOAT
SERGEANT! WAKE UP!!
WHAT'S GOING ON, SERGEANT ?!

Ge... gero... IT'S... NOTHING.
I JUST KINDA LOST MY BALANCE, AND...FELL DOWN. THAT'S ALL.
BY THE WAY, MASTER FUYUKI... WHAT ABOUT THAT GUNDAM MODEL I ASKED FOR?
I'M SORRY, SERGEANT. I WASN'T ABLE TO FIND IT.
I SEE.

WELL, AGGAI IS PRETTY POPULAR...
......
DON'T WORRY, I'LL DO YOUR CHORES TODAY. YOU JUST STAY IN BED AND GET BETTER.
THANK YOU, MASTER FUYUKI.

HOW CAN HE BE SICK?
HE IS A LIVING CREATURE, YOU KNOW.

THE PROBLEM IS, HE'S NOT FROM EARTH...
IF AN ALIEN FALLS ILL HERE ON EARTH, OUR MEDICINES MAY NOT WORK ON HIM.
I WONDER IF WE CAN HELP AT ALL...
kata kata

kata

EH. I BET HE'LL BE BETTER IN NO TIME.
MAYBE KULULU WILL COME UP WITH SOME-THING!
I HOPE YOU'RE RIGHT...

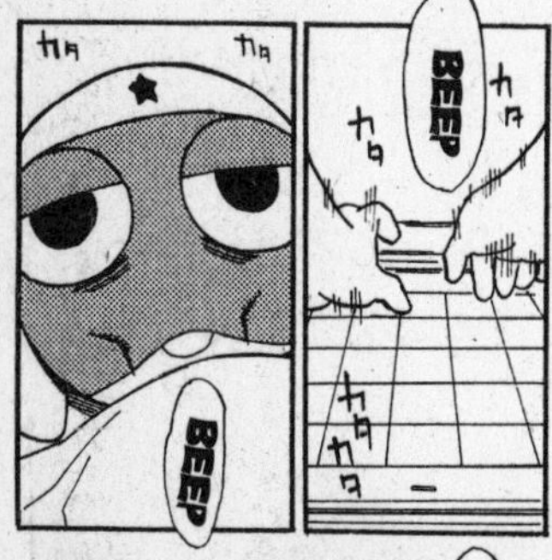
BEEP
BEEP

BEEE
BOOOOP

UNKNOWN... NO KNOWN CASES EXIST.
I GUESS THE CAPTAIN GETS THE HONOR OF BEING NUMBER ONE...WHAT LUCK!
I'LL CONTINUE THE ANALYSIS, BUT...
...DON'T EXPECT TOO MUCH. IT'S NOT MY SPECIALTY, YOU KNOW...
G-Gero... I KNOW YOU, KULULU.
YOU ALWAYS COME THROUGH... EVEN WHEN IT SEEMS THERE'S NO HOPE...
Ku...
...I SEE.
SO...I AM DISEASED...
WELL, I SUPPOSE MY GUNDAM MODEL FEVER IS KIND OF LIKE A DISEASE, TOO! ♪
AH HA HA HA HA HA!
AH HA HA HA HA... HA...
......

UNCLE!!!
AH! LADY MOA.
YOU'RE JUST IN TIME. I WAS JUST CONTEMPLATING THE LONELINESS THAT IS CRUSHING MY...
LEAP
Gerooo ?!!
I HEARD THE PROGNOSIS!!
PLEASE DON'T DIE, UNCLE!
EH? DEATH?!!
IF I WERE TO LOSE YOU, I...I...!
NO...WAIT, LADY MOA!
I'M ABOUT TO BE LOST BY A DIFFERENT MEANS!!
CRUSH
CRACK!

IF UNCLE MUST GO...
...SO MUST THIS ENTIRE PLANET!!!
BUT--! BUT--! LADY MOA!
E-EARTHQUAKES ARE CONSIDERED A NUISANCE TO SOCIETY! REMEMBER ?!
FEAR NOT, UNCLE.
ANGOL MOA'S JUDGMENT DAY ATTIRE
Design assistance by Okana
THE APOCALYPTIC ARMAGEDDON GENERATED BY THIS RITUAL OUTFIT WILL ANNIHILATE THE PLANET WITHOUT ELASTIC UNDULATION *!
IT WILL BE A MERCIFUL END.
NOW, HOLD STILL...THIS WON'T HURT A BIT.
*Commonly known as an earthquake.

APOCALYPSE
NOW!!!
YEEEK! I DON'T WANNA DIE!!
!
PLIK
HAH...? LADY MOA?
SHUUU...
PHEW. THAT WAS TOO CLOSE
gasp
gasp
FORGIVE ME, LADY MOA.
DORORO! MASTER KOYUKI!
WHAT'S GOING ON?
EH HEH HEH!♪ WE CAME TO COMFORT YOU, KERORO-SAN!
Phew!
WELL, GREAT TIMING!

SORRY, UNCLE...I WAS...HOW DO YOU SAY... CARRIED AWAY?
しゅん…
THINK NOTHING OF IT, LADY MOA. ♪
shucks
IT SEEMS THAT THE CAPTAIN'S DISEASE STILL IS YET TO BE DIAGNOSED ...
LEAVE THAT TO THE SHINOBI!
TA-DAHHH! KOYUKI AZUMA'S SPECIAL BLEND: HYOROHGAN!!
THIS'LL CURE WHAT AILS YOU IN NO TIME! ♪
I HELPED, TOO!
どん!
KINDA... BLACK, ISN'T IT?
NEVER MIND ABOUT THE COLOR. NOW...OPEN WIIIDE!
AAAH ...
DROP
OOPS.
SORRY. I DROPPED IT!
...PRETTY HEAVY, ISN'T IT?
TAKES YOU BACK, DOESN'T IT, KERORO-KUN?
HEH?

REMEMBER? I WAS RATHER SICKLY MYSELF AS A CHILD.
OUR ROLES HAVE MERELY BEEN REVERSED.
Gero... YOU THINK...?

BUT...
BUT ...???

YOU NEVER VISITED ME, KERORO-KUN.
I COULD HEAR ALL OF YOU PLAYING IN THE PARK... EVERY SINGLE DAY.

IT WAS SO LONELY...
どんより。

WELL, GOTTA GO!
TAKE CARE OF YOURSELF, Y'HEAR?
ひゅっ
qucik
exit
散ッ

W-WELL...
LOTTA GUESTS TODAY, EH?
GLACK
I'M SORRY, UNCLE.

*In other words, his manga needs an entire rewrite.

SERGEANT...
I'LL LOOK A FEW OTHER PLACES, OKAY...?

AW, NUTS!
THAT STUPID BROAD GOT HERE BEFORE ME!
DOGGONE THAT WOMAN. TAKING ADVANTAGE OF MISTER SERGEANT IN HIS WEAKENED STATE...
NOT ON MY WATCH! I'M GOING TO WIN BUNCH OF POINTS WITH HIM RIGHT NOW!!

DUMB HUSSY... I'M SURE HE'S TIRED OF HER COMPANY ALREADY...
BUT CANDY AND GUNDAMS AND OTHER MATERIAL THINGS...THAT STUFF NEVER GETS OLD!
Go, go, Uncle!
Go, Uncle!
OH MISTER SERGEANT, SIRRRR!!
PRIVATE TAMAMA, REPORTING FOR VISIT!
!?

Zzzz
Zzzz
SHHH
whisper
whisper
YOU'LL WAKE UNCLE UP.

whisper
HE JUST FELL ASLEEP...
whisper
PLEASE BE QUIET...FOR HIM, TAMA-CHAN.
whisper
whisper
M- MY ELECTRO-LYTIC QUOTIENT HAS BEEN REDUCED TO...
...THE LAXITY OF DAMAGED HAIR...
SPEAKING ABSOLUTE GIBBERISH.

WHAT?!
WHAT DO YOU MEAN, YOU CAN'T TELL ME?!
I told you a bunch of times! You can't go get him a Space Keruperos this time!
Because of over-hunting, they've been desig-nated as an endangered species !!

ARRRGH! ALL RIGHT!!

HOW COULD HE GET SICK AT A TIME LIKE THIS?!
IF HE DOESN'T TAKE COMMAND, WHO WILL...?
GRUMPLE
INVASION PLAN

KERORO...

Otaku Mania

I FOUND IT...!
BUT...
MACROSS

IT'S PROBABLY...
...ALREADY BEEN RESERVED.

UM, EXCUSE ME. THAT AGGAI...
IT'S RESERVED, KID. I CAN'T SELL IT TO YOU.

JUST AS I THOUGHT...
HEY, MAN. MY AGGAI IN YET?
OH, YES. IT'S HERE.

OH, HEY! WHAT'S UP, FUYUKI-KUN?
WHA...?

MUTSUMI-SAN!!
WHAT ARE YOU DOING ALL THE WAY OUT IN SHIBUYA?

SERGEANT! I GOT IT!
I GOT YOU YOUR AGGAI!!

SER--
SERGEANT...?

N-NO!
SERGEANT !!!
WHAT IS IT, MASTER FUYUKI?
HERE, LET ME CHANGE THAT WASH-CLOTH FOR YOU. ♪
MOA-CHAN! YOU DON'T PUT IT ON LIKE THAT!!

SHEESH! DON'T SCARE ME LIKE THAT!
SO, LOOKS LIKE YOU'RE DOING OKAY, THEN?
WELL... NOT QUITE.
HUH?

WE STILL DON'T KNOW THE CAUSE OF HIS DISEASE, OR EVEN WHAT DISEASE IT IS...
Um...Lady Moa? I don't think this is quite right either...
huff
I-it isn't?
huff huff
HIS TEMPERATURE CONTINUES TO RISE... HE'S GROWING WEAKER BY THE MINUTE... IN OTHER WORDS... HE'S GETTING WORSE.

BUT-- CAN'T YOU DO ANY-THING?!
NO. WE MUST LET IT RUN ITS COURSE.
EXOTIC ILLNESS IS AN UN-AVOIDABLE RISK...
...THAT ALL INTER-STELLAR INVADERS MUST FACE.
GIRORO...

OH? GIRORO?
I'M GLAD YOU'RE HERE.
THAT GREAT SCHEME WE TALKED ABOUT AT THE MEETING...
IF SOME-THING SHOULD... HAPPEN... TO ME...

...PLEASE TAKE CHARGE IN MY PLACE.
......?!!
N-NO! YOU IDIOT!!!
shred
shred
YOU'RE THE CAPTAIN !!
IF YOU CAN'T LEAD US, WHO WILL?!!
OH...
SER-GEANT !!
MISTER SER-GEANT, SIR!
UNCLE !!!
KERORO !!
THEN... HE'S GOING TO...
...NO. IT CAN'T BE!
DING-DONG

I'M HOOOME! ♪
SO? HOW'S KERO-CHAN DOING?
Er...
OH...? NOT SO WELL?
WE'LL HAVE TO HURRY, THEN. ♪
SOMIT
WILL YOU HELP ME, NATSUMI?
HUH?
EVERYONE... CALM DOWN, PLEASE!
HEH...I CAN'T EVEN GET SICK WITHOUT CREATING A RUCKUS...!
S-SORRY...
BUT...I APPRECIATE ALL OF YOUR GOODWILL.
I AM A FORTUNATE FROG INDEED!
KNOCK KNOCK

KERO-CHAN! HOW ARE YOU DOING?
GENERAL MOM!
HERE. I BOUGHT SOMETHING FOR YOU!
HEH?
CLOSE YOUR EYES FOR A SECOND, OKAY?
NOW... OPEN WIIIIDE... ♥
AHHHHHH!
BITE

WH-WHAT KIND OF THING DID YOU JUST STUFF INTO ME...?
WHAT KIND OF...
S-SERGEANT...!
slob slob slob slob

IT'S... DELICIOUS!!!
SUPER! FINE! YUMMY! GOOD!!
He's...flying?
U-UNCLE IS...
HE'S ALL BETTER!!!

IS THIS A POKOPENIAN PLANT?
I PEELED IT FOR HIM, YOU KNOW.
WHOA! IT'S IN THE SHAPE OF A STAR!
STAR FRUIT, ALSO KNOWN AS STAR APPLE. NATIVE TO THE TROPICS. WHEN CUT CROSS-WISE, IT RESEMBLES A STAR.
THE TASTE IS...WELL, NORMAL... BUT...
THE TEXTURE IS VERY RE-FRESHING! IT'S LIKE A TROPICAL BREEZE BLOWING THROUGH YOUR WHOLE BODY!
IT'S NOT A VERY POPULAR FRUIT HERE ON EARTH, BUT I THOUGHT IT MIGHT BE PERFECT FOR YOU, KERO-CHAN.
HOW DO YOU LIKE IT?
Oho! Taha!
REALLY? I'M SO GLAD.
Ku ku ku... THIS IS A SURPRISE.
THIS IS A POKOPENIAN PLANT...BUT SOMEHOW, IT CONTAINS A HIGH CONCENTRATION OF KERONIAN PLANET ESSENCE...
...IN OTHER WORDS, IT'S THE PERFECT NUTRITIONAL SUPPLEMENT FOR OUR CAPTAIN...
OH, REALLY?
Right on, mom!
Mmm! It's good!
EVERYBODY! I'M SO SORRY TO HAVE MADE YOU WORRY!
SERGEANT KERORO IS BACK ON DUTY!!!
FIT AS A FIDDLE!

I'M SO GLAD, SER-GEANT!!
BUT...WHAT KIND OF DISEASE WAS IT?

OH...
WELL, HEATSTROKE, RIGHT?

EH ...?
Gero ?!
HE HAD ALL THE TYPICAL SYMPTOMS.
ANYTHING ELSE YOU CAN THINK OF, KERO-CHAN?

GERO? WELL... YESTERDAY, OR PERHAPS THE DAY BEFORE...
I WAS WORKING ON GUNDAM MODELS AND PLAYING SOME GAMES... THEN I WORKED ON MORE MODELS... THEN SURFED THE NET...
Did I eat?
Did I sleep?
...THEN, WHEN I WAS DONE FILLING OUT THAT ITEM COLUMN, IT WAS MORNING, SO I WENT STRAIGHT TO THE MEETING...!
EH...?

SHEESH! WHY WERE WE ALL SO WORRIED?!!
KERORO-- WHY, YOU--!!
YOU'RE AN IDIOT, MISTER SERGEANT, SIR.
OH, UNCLE ...
Meh ...
...well, maybe I'll take back the Aggai.
Gero?! WHATEVER HAPPENED TO LOYALTY?!
PROPER NUTRITION... PLENTY OF EXERCISE... ADEQUATE REST. ALL YOU EARTH ALIENS, TAKE CARE NOW, Y'HEAR?
TO BE CONTINUED

ONE DAY, DURING A WEEK OF PARTICU-LARLY OPPRESSIVE HEAT...
THANK YOU!

....A WONDER-FUL GIFT ARRIVED!
WATER-MELONS FROM GRANDMA!!
SUMMER 723
ENCOUNTER XCV ALL HAIL THE WATERMELON GENERATION
YEAH! GRANDMA'S WATERMELONS ARE ALWAYS SO SWEET AND JUICY!
NOT TO MENTION GREAT FOR ONE'S HEALTH AND BEAUTY!
Just look at Mom! ♡
WHY DON'T WE HAVE SOME RIGHT NOW?
YEAH! LET'S HAVE SOME NOW!!
Ooh! Ooh!

*In memory of the Japanese Comedy group The Drifters, 1964–2004. Respect.

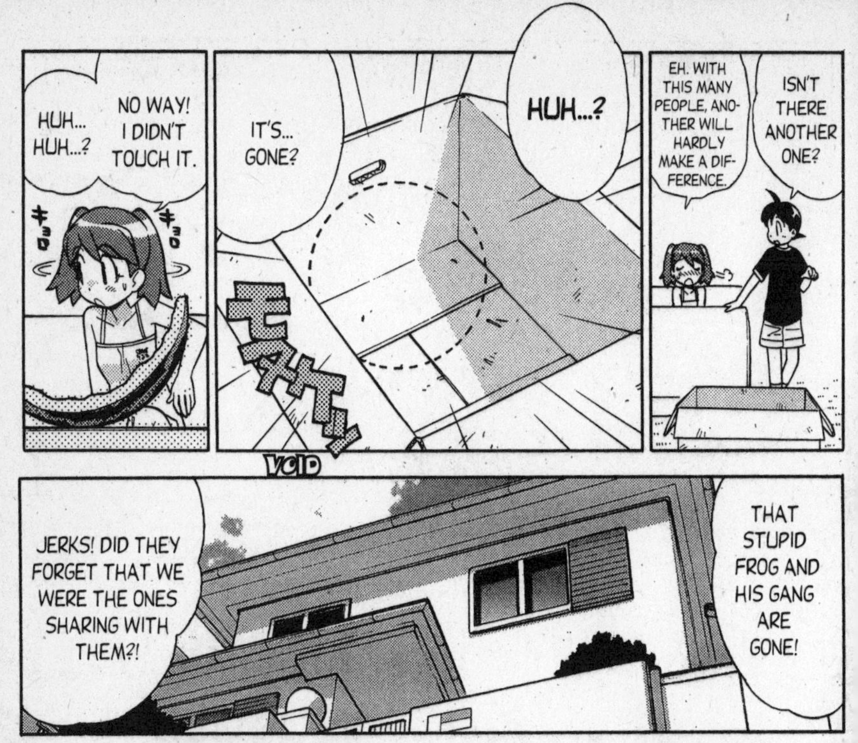
ISN'T THERE ANOTHER ONE?
EH. WITH THIS MANY PEOPLE, ANOTHER WILL HARDLY MAKE A DIFFERENCE.
HUH...?
IT'S... GONE?
NO WAY! I DIDN'T TOUCH IT.
HUH... HUH...?
VOID
THAT STUPID FROG AND HIS GANG ARE GONE!
JERKS! DID THEY FORGET THAT WE WERE THE ONES SHARING WITH THEM?!

STUPID FROG!!
Gero Gero Gero! THAT MASTER NATSUMI! HOW GREEDY!

POKOPENIANS ARE TERRIBLE AT STRETCHING OUT LIMITED RESOURCES.
SERGEANT MAJOR KULULU!
Ku ku ku ku!
BEEP
BEEP

LEAVE IT TO ME...

IT'S ALL RIGHT, NATSUMI!
WE'LL JUST ASK GRANDMA TO SEND US ANOTHER ONE.
THAT'S NOT THE POINT!!

HE WOULD'VE EATEN IT ALL BY HIMSELF IF HE COULD!
I'll never forgive him.
KNOCK KNOCK
KNOCK KNOCK
KNOCK KNOCK
Come Come
KNOCK KNOCK
WHAT DO YOU MEAN, COMING BACK LIKE THIS?!
HAVE YOU NO...
... SHAME?
WHAT ARE YOU DOING?! THAT'S OUR WATER-MELON!
Gero Gero!! YOU CLOSED-MINDED POKOPENIANS COULDN'T EVEN IMAGINE SOME-THING LIKE THIS!

HEY...IS THAT... BIGGER THAN IT WAS BEFORE?
YES, MASTER FUYUKI! GOOD EYE!
I'VE IMPROVED IT TO ABSORB WATER AND GROW EVEN BIGGER...
...ALL WHILE MAINTAINING ITS GOOD-TASTING CHARACTERISTICS SOON, WE WILL ALL EAT TO OUR HEARTS' DELIGHT...!
SHAAAAH

A GIFT TO YOU, IN EXCHANGE FOR THE SWEET AND DELICIOUS WATERMELON YOU SHARED WITH US!!
I SHALL SHOUT IT OUT, LOUD AND CLEAR!
GREETINGS TO YOU, THIS HOT SUMMER DAY!!
ぱぁあ!

SO THAT'S IT! SERGEANT, YOU REALLY WERE THINKING OF US!
YUP! NOW WE CAN ALL ENJOY IT UNTIL OUR TUMMIES ARE FULL!
ぱぁあぁあ
Though I was the one who really wanted more...
ALL RIGHT, ALL RIGHT. I'M SORRY I DOUBTED YOU.
IF THAT'S THE CASE, THEN I'LL GLADLY...
?! HEY! WHAT THE...
ぐん...
ぐぐん...
ISN'T THAT TOO BIG?
?

UNCLE!! THE WATERMELON'S "YUMMY IN MY TUMMY" FACTOR IS OFF THE CHARTS AND RISING!
VOOOOM
Can't live
Can't move
Maybe I'll save some
Well pleased
Just so
Want more
IT'S COMPLETELY SURPASSED ITS TARGET VALUE! LIKE, PRIZE-WINNING CROP?!
AH! IT SEEMS IT'S READY TO EAT NOW!
WE JUST NEED TO TURN OFF THE WATER...
SLITHER
EH...?
BREAK
WHOA! THE RESTRAINING STRAP!!!
OUT OF CONTROL!!!
RE-STRAINING STRAP? ISN'T THAT JUST A FRUIT CAP?
WELL... WE WERE USING IT TO RESTRICT THE GROWTH OF THE WATER-MELON...
THAT'S WEIRD. I ADJUSTED IT FOR POKOPENAIN FRUIT...
Did I err?
WHA?
KULULU! WATER-MELON ISN'T A FRUIT!!
IT'S A VEGETABLE!!!
I...I DIDN'T KNOW... GYAAAA!!
IT'S...
PEEL
... FLYING ...?!!

WAAAAAAAAH!
I DON'T WANT TO DIE SQUASHED BY A WATER-MELON!!
FOOOOM!
SUPPLY HOSE (ACCIDEN-TALLY) SEVERED!
WATER-MELON IS SETTLING DOWN!
WE'RE... SAVED...
NOW HOW THE HECK ARE WE SUP-POSED TO EAT THIS?!
ARE YOU GUYS EVEN CAPABLE OF NOT CAUSING TROUBLE?!
TAP TAP
HEY...IT SOUNDS PRETTY GOOD!
EH...?
GREAT COLOR AND SHINE, TOO! THIS'LL BE REALLY GOOD TO EAT! ♪
No way...

TO BE CONTINUED

THE SEASON WHEN COSMOS FLOWERS BLOOM...
OOH...HOW CUTE! ♪
ENCOUNTER XCVI
CRASH! TYPHOON DECLARES VICTORY!
SO, AKIZAKURA, OR "FALL CHERRY BLOSSOM," ARE ALSO CALLED COSMOS...
A MIGHTY WIND...
EH? WHAT'S SO SPECIAL ABOUT IT? CAN IT DOUBLE AS FOOD AND FIREARM?
IDIOT.
THEY'RE PRETTY. DON'T YOU THINK?
KOYUKI-CHAN GAVE THEM TO ME. ♡
That little --?!
WHA?!
...IS COMING.
KYA!

ENCOUNTER XCVI
CRASH! TYPHOON DECLARES VICTORY!

Though it was not previously certain that typhoon K would make landfall...
...it seems to have made up its mind. Typhoon K is indeed forecast to hit Japan this afternoon.
Its strength is still fluctuating, so please stay tuned and be prepared for any-thing.
HEH... WHAT A STRANGE TYPHOON.
IT'S ACTUALLY KIND OF LIKE YOU, SERGEANT!

REALLY? THEN IT MUST BE A WELL-RESPECTED, DISTINGUISHED, NICE TYPHOON THAT LOOKS GOOD IN GREEN!
EH...?

SER-GEANT ...DON'T YOU KNOW ABOUT TY-PHOONS?
OH, QUITE!

UH... Y'SEE, A TYPHOON IS...
!!
AND AT THAT VERY MOMENT, SOME-THING DAWNED ON THE BOY!

Gero?
OH, UH... NEVER MIND!

GOOD! PRE-ASSEMBLE: COM-PLETE!!
I SHALL FINALIZE ASSEMBLY IN MY QUARTERS!
Sigh...

CLACK
PHEW... THAT WAS CLOSE.
WOULDN'T WANT HIM TO GO, "GERO GERO. I CAN USE THIS FOR OUR INVASION!"
IT'S A TYPHOON, NOT A JOKE!

...I GUESS I SHOULD CLOSE THE SHUTTERS.
SLIDE
SLIDE
WHOA!!

Gero Gero Gero Gero...

THE SERGEANT'S INTUITION FOR INVASION OPPORTU-NITIES IS UN-PARALLELED!!

I'M SUPPOSED TO BE A PROUD SOLDIER OF THE KERON FORCES!

BUT LOOK AT ME NOW!

I'M THE ONE HOLDING BACK THE POKOPEN INVASION...!!

WELL, DUH!

RUMBLE RUMBLE

CLICK
PELT
PELT
PELT
SLAM!
RATTLE
RATTLE
HHHZZZ
IT'S REALLY COMING DOWN NOW!
I WONDER IF THIS TYPHOON'S GONNA BE A REALLY BAD ONE...
バラ
バラ
バラ
バラ
バラ

EEEEH ...!
I CAN'T GO HOOOME...
FEAR NOT, YOUNG MAN.
LEAVE IT TO ME!

*Another word for typhoon.

KERORO PLATOON'S UNDERGROUND BASE
KULULU!!
DID A PACKAGE ARRIVE FOR ME?!
WHERE?! WHERE IS IT?!
over there
OOOOOOOOOH!!
"SUPER INVASION WEAPON: TEMPEST GRADE"!!
I DIDN'T THINK I'D EVER BE ABLE TO GET ONE...
Whoa! I did it!
...BUT IT WAS COMPLETELY WORTH SENDING AWAY TO *SPACE WEAPONS MONTHLY'S* READER SWEEPSTAKES EVERY MONTH!
WITH THIS...
...I CAN TAKE POKOPEN SINGLE-HANDEDLY!!!
IF YOU HAD JUST ASKED, I WOULD HAVE MADE ONE FOR YOU...
Ku ku ku
M-MIND YOUR OWN BUSINESS!

NOW THE ONLY QUESTION IS... WHERE TO USE IT.
THIS IS A STRATEGIC WEAPON, WITH AN "SS" DANGER LEVEL...

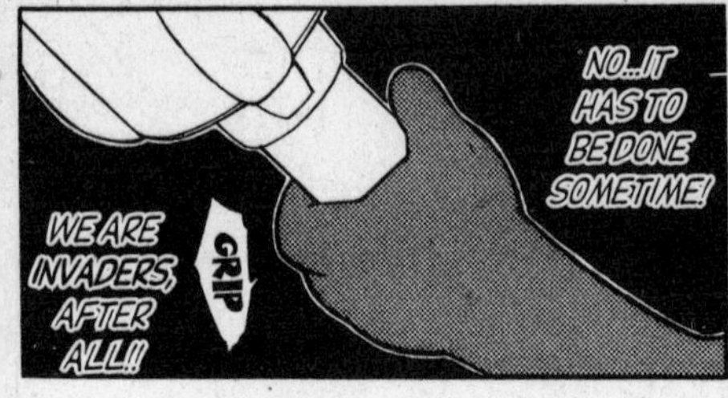
NO...IT HAS TO BE DONE SOMETIME!
WE ARE INVADERS, AFTER ALL!!
GRIP

YOU DON'T NEED ANYTHING LIKE THAT... RIGHT NOW...
ガーッ
EH? WHAT'S THAT? WHAT'S THAT?!

WHOA! DUDE! TIGHT!
スチャッ
CAN I SHOOT IT?!
N-NO! STOP!!

THIS IS NOT A TOY!
DO YOU WANT TO BLOW US ALL AWAY?!!
AW, SHOOT. JERK!
ばしっ

WELL, LET'S JUST LEAVE THE WRINKLY RED DEMON TO HIS OWN...
KULULU! I HAVE A VERY IMPORTANT QUESTION!

WHAT IS THIS... TYPHOON?
Ku...

ウォン
ウォン
WELL, A TYPHOON IS WHAT POKO-PENIANS CALL A "NATURAL DISASTER."
IT CANNOT BE CONTROLLED WITH THE LIMITED KNOWLEDGE OF POKOPEN.
ウォン
ウォン
Gero Gero... WHAT AN INEPT BUNCH!
UNDERGROUND BASE SIMULATOR ROOM
BY LISTENING TO THE TYPHOON'S FEELINGS, WE CAN GET INSIDE ITS HEAD AND MASTER ITS CONTROL! YES, WE CAN USE THIS "TYPHOON" MOST EFFECTIVELY!
Hup! two three four
SERGEANT MAJOR KULULU! I'M READY!!
Two! two three four
AYE-AYE... CAPTAIN ...
PUSH
Ku ku ku... SIMULATION: ON!
CLANK
THIS CLASSIFIES AS A "POWERFUL, LARGE-SCALE TYPHOON."
HMMM...I SEE.
rattle rattle
Gero Gero... NOT VERY IMPRESSIVE, IS IT?

VERY WELL. THIS IS A "VERY POWERFUL, LARGE-SCALE TYPHOON."
HMMM... QUITE NICE...!
WITH THIS, THE POKOPENIANS WON'T DARE GET IN OUR WAY!!
I...I CAN'T OPEN MY EYES!
THIS IS AN "EVEN MORE POWERFUL, LARGE-SCALE TYPHOON."
GOOD GOD, MAN!!
THIS IS DANGEROUS!! I'M GOING TO GET HURT!!
AND THIS IS THE "FURIOUS LARGE-SCALE TYPHOON!"
UP NEXT IS A "FURIOUS, SUPER LARGE-SCALE"... HUH...? CAPTAIN?
SO...THIS IS WHAT A TYPHOON IS LIKE.
WELL... MORE OR LESS.

THIS IS A PHENOMENON NEVER SEEN ON PLANETS LIKE OURS, WHERE SCIENCE IS MORE ADVANCED...
DON'T WORRY, 556--I'M HERE!
ON POKOPEN, EVERY TIME THIS HAPPENS, THE ACTIVITIES OF HUMANS BECOME GREATLY LIMITED...
AND IT SEEMS THAT ONE OF THESE **TYPHOONS** IS ON ITS WAY... **RIGHT NOW**.
IF WE USE YOUR T-GRADE...
...POKOPEN INVASION WILL BE A CINCH...
H-HUMPH! THAT'S UP TO KERORO, NOT YOU!
HE IS THE CAPTAIN, AFTER ALL...

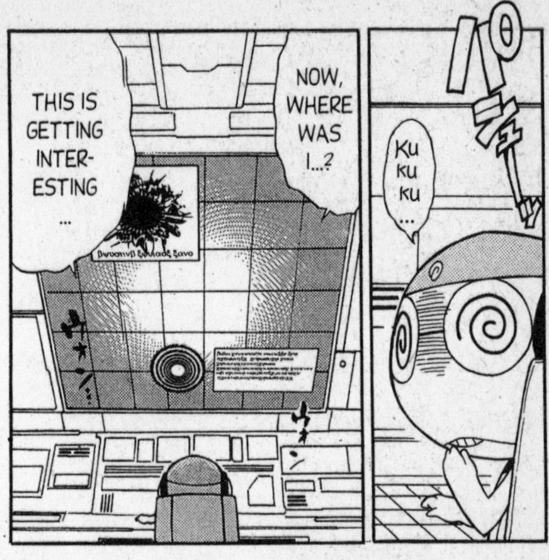
Ku ku ku ...
NOW, WHERE WAS I...?
THIS IS GETTING INTER-ESTING ...

CLICK
NO WORRIES, MOM! THE SHUTTERS ARE CLOSED.
CLICK CLICK CLICK
AND WE HAVE LEFTOVERS FOR DINNER!

OH, DEAR. LOOKS LIKE IT'S GETTING WORSE...
YOU TAKE CARE, OKAY, NA-TSUMI?
Okay, Mom. You, too!

I WONDER IF MOM'LL BE ABLE TO COME HOME...
BEEP
DUNNO. THE TRAINS MIGHT STOP RUNNING.

THOSE COSMOS FLOWERS THAT KOYUKI GAVE ME...
...I WONDER IF THEY'LL SURVIVE.
Sigh...

YOU MUST BE OUT OF YOUR MIND!
IF WE TRY TO INVADE AT A TIME LIKE THIS, WE'LL BE DEAD IN NO TIME!!
ON A DAY LIKE THIS, ONE SHOULD STAY PUT, AND...YOU KNOW.
WORK ON GUNDAM MODELS OR SOMETHING! THAT'S THE PRUDENT COURSE OF ACTION!
Ow ow ow!
Hmm... powerful large-scale typhoon "K" looks like...
...it certainly will make landfall in Shizuoka.

WELL KNOWN FOR ITS MODEL-MAKING INDUSTRY...
SHIZUOKA
SHIZUOKA HOBBY SHOW
...AND ITS TEA...
...AND... ITS GUNDAM MODELS!

I WON'T ALLOW IT!
SER-GEANT ?!
RIGHT NOW, THIS MAN IS THE EYE OF THE STORM!
TY-PHOON !!!
I WON'T LET YOU HAVE YOUR WAY WITH THE HARD-WORKING INDUSTRIES OF SHIZUOKA!!!
WITH THE TROPICAL LOW PRESSURE, THE "KERORO FROM BACK THEN" IS BACK IN ACTION!
KYAAAA?!
WIND!! CLOUDS!! LIGHTNING!!!
SER-GEANT ??!
I SHALL BE THE SOLE SAVIOR OF THE PLASTIC MODEL INDUSTRY!!!

URRGH! WHAT THE HECK IS HE THINKING?!!
WHAT'S GOING ON?
GIRORO!
HE WENT FLYING OUT INTO THE STORM!
WHAT THE...?!
THAT IDIOT!!
THIS IS THE OPPORTUNE TIME FOR POKOPEN INVASION, AND...!!

Mew? Mew?
COME.
YOU'LL BE SAFE HERE.
STAY HERE, ALL RIGHT?!

BEEP

The little typhoon that originated in Japan appears to have gone out...
...and collided with the larger typhoon "K."
I've never seen this happen--have you, Morita-san?
Oh! The little typhoon has disappeared!
FFT!
COULD THAT... MAYBE... BE THE STUPID FROG...?

Target confirmed. Moving towards circular object at top speed.
We are now entering an area of high winds.
WHAT IS THAT IDIOT DOING?!
Target apprehended.
!!

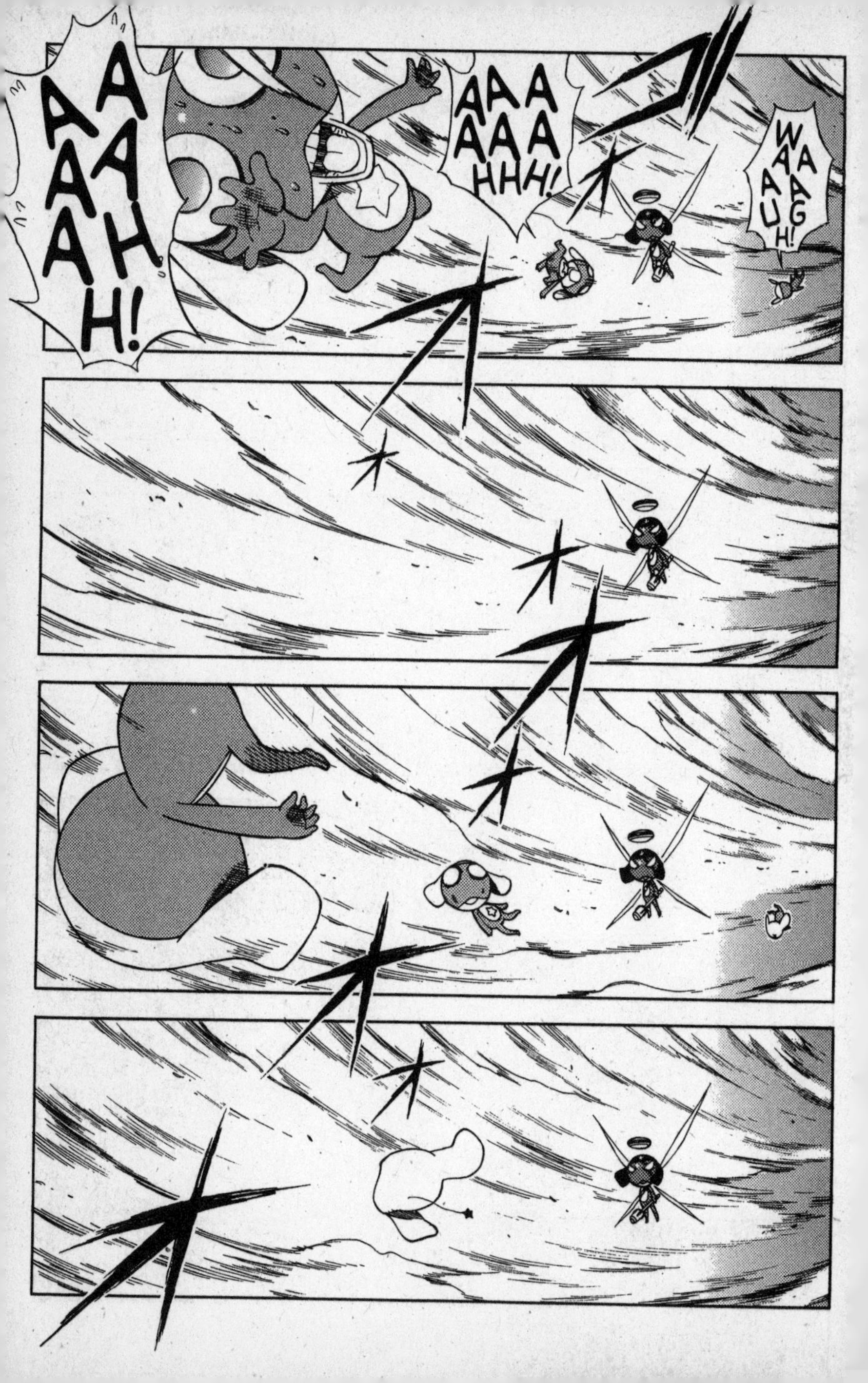
WAAAAUGH!
AAAAAAHHH!
AAAAAHH!

WHAT IS HE DOING?!
OPER-ATION:
POKOPEN INVASION.
NOOOO!

PLOP

IF WE USE YOUR T-GRADE...
...INVADING POKOPEN WILL BE A CINCH...
KA-SHUK

ゴオオオ
SHOOM
KA-CLACK!
WHAT GIRORO JUST SHOT INTO THE EYE OF THE TYPHOON WAS A T-GRADE CLIMACTIC WEAPON.
FOR HIGHLY EVOLVED CIVILIZATIONS THAT CAN CONTROL WEATHER, IT IS A WEAPON OF ULTIMATE POWER.

BEFORE GIRORO SHOT THAT WEAPON INTO THE TYPHOON'S EYE, HE SET THE AGGRAVATION VECTOR TO "CLOCKWISE."
WHICH MEANS...
GO-OH!

Unbelievable! The typhoon has completely dissipated!
Update: Strange weather patterns seem to be occurring one after another!
Whoa...
...HUH?
OOH, WHAT LUCK!
LOOKS LIKE I'LL BE ABLE TO GO HOME AFTER ♪ ALL.
PHEW ...
THAT WAS CLOSE.

NARUTO ONE TO SUKARU ONE.
OFFENSIVE COMPLETE. RETURNING TO BASE.

PLEASE NOTE THAT IN THIS INSTANCE, WE PRIORITIZED THE SAFETY OF THE CAPTAIN OVER THE INVASION.
Sigh...
THOUGH REGRETTABLY...
Ku ku... AYE-AYE.

DESPITE WHAT I SAID EARLIER...
I GUESS IT WAS THE RIGHT THING TO DO, SIR...
What was that?

...these guys on Pokopen have been at it against typhoons since the beginning of time.
We would have to be pretty lucky to invade so easily...
Ku ku ku...

IT'S SO NICE OUT NOW--AS IF IT NEVER HAPPENED!
はっ
THAT'S RIGHT!
KOYUKI'S COSMOS!
ぱシャ
ぱシャ

THEY'RE OKAY!!

This just in: Another typhoon appears to be on its way.
Please take the neces-sary pre-cautions, and stay tuned...
SERGEANT, DON'T EVEN THINK ABOUT INVADING EARTH AGAIN!
N-NO WAY, JOSE!
NEVER!!
ガタガタ
ブルブル
TO BE CONTINUED

*A grand trick where you turn the rope three times in a single jump.♡

I'M JUMPING ROPE, 'CAUSE WE'VE GOT A JUMP ROPE TEST IN P.E. TOMORROW, REMEMBER?!
YOU SHOULD BE JUMPING ROPE, TOO!
NO MATTER HOW WELL YOU DO IT... IT WON'T GET YOU TO SPACE.
Not very athletic...
WHY DO WE JUMP ROPE AT ALL? HOW CAN IT POSSIBLY BENEFIT OUR EXISTENCE ??
LONG PAST MAKING A FALSE CHARGE, FUYUKI HAS ENTERED THE REALM OF SURREAL!
JUST YOU WAIT...I'LL CONQUER THAT TRIPLE JUMP!
JUMP ROPE...
YAAAH!!
SLAP!
HAAAAH...
URRGH... IT'S DRIVING ME MAD!
hah hah
NATSUMI-CHAN!!
I SEE YOU'RE DEEP IN THE MIDST OF TRAINING!
BUT IT'S MUCH MORE FUN TO TRAIN TOGETHER!!
THE ARMY OF THE SHADOWS!
FORSOOTH!
KOYUKI-CHAN! DORORO!
tmp
tmp

ROPE WORK IS ONE OF THE FOUNDATIONS OF NINJA TRAINING!
IT DOES WONDERS FOR ONE'S HEALTH AND BEAUTY!
REALLY?
LET'S BEGIN WITH THE ART OF ESCAPE!
NO, NO, NO... YOU'RE USING IT ALL WRONG!
YOU JUST JUMP OVER IT... NORMALLY
...HUH?
OH, I SEE. IT'S LIKE JUMPING ROPE. ♬
Y-YES.
SO MUCH WORK FOR THAT SIMPLE RESPONSE ...
OH, HEY, KOYUKI-CHAN! LET'S DO AYATOBI. ♪
AYATOBI?
SURE. LET'S DO IT TOGETHER! ♪
ONE, TWO...
THREE!
JUMP!
IRIS

HMM... MASTER KOYUKI ISN'T HALF BAD.
Whoa...
DORORO!
HURRICANE
HAAH !!
I CAN'T LET HER UP-STAGE ME!

HOW WAS I?
OH, DEAR. MY APOLOGIES, MASTER NATSUMI.
...CAN WE PLEASE JUST DO THIS THE REGULAR WAY?

YES... THAT'S RIGHT! ♪
REGULAR, BUT NOT ORDINARY! I SEE!
THIS IS SO MUCH FUN, NAT-SUMI-CHAN! ♡
I'M HAVING FUN, TOO, KOYUKI-CHAN!
Ah ha ha ha! Eeek Eeek!
I JUST DON'T GET THIS AT ALL.
HEY, SOUNDS FUN! CAN I PLAY, TOO?
WHAT'S ALL THE RUCKUS?
UGH...TWO POTENTIAL COMPLI-CATIONS.

OOH! A CHANCE FOR ME TO SHOW OFF!
D-DO I HAVE TO DO THIS, TOO?!
HOOOOOH...

Ha-yaah! Ho-yaah!
Ho-waaah!
Aye Aye Aye Aye Ahhh!
OH-AH-CHAAAH!
OH-AH-CHAAAH?!

WOO! I'M SORRY.
ALWAYS PRACTICE SAFETY WITH JUMP ROPES! ESPECIALLY THE VINYL ONES...
SOB...!
DON'T WORRY! I'LL TEACH YOU!
LET'S ALL DO IT... NORMALLY!
YEAH!!

DAAAH DAAAH ♪ DAAAHDEE DA DAAAH DEE DA ♪ DAAAH
DEEE DEEE DEEE DEEE ♫ ♪ DA DEEE DEEE DA DAAAH ♫
No... Any-one but him!
HERALDED BY DARTH VADER'S INFAMOUS IMPERIAL MARCH...
... SER-GEANT KERORO COMETH!!!
Y'ALL AREN'T HAVIN' FUN WITHOUT ME NOW, ARE YA?
Gooh... Hooh...

WHAT YOU'RE DOING...THIS IS CALLED... ROPE-LEAPING, YES?
HOW FOOLISH OF YOU TO LEAP ROPE WITHOUT ME...
UM... "LEAP ROPE"?
BACK THEN, AFTER WEEKS OF ENDLESS TRAINING, I WAS CROWNED THE "KING OF THE ROPE LEAP!"
AND THE TRICK I DEVISED--AND MASTERED--WAS THE APTLY NAMED "QUINTUPLE LEAP!!"
QUIN-TUPLE ?!

NO WAY! IT'S IMPOS-SIBLE TO DO A QUIN-TUPLE!
Gero Gero...
YOU ARE ONLY SHOWING YOUR OWN LIMITS.
THEN WHY DON'T YOU SHOW ME!
HEH HEH HEH... GLADLY.
HAND IT OVER ...
...BEFORE YOU HURT YOUR-SELF.
MASTER NATSU-MI!
IT SEEMS THAT YOU DON'T BELIEVE IN YOURSELF... BUT!

TO BELIEVE YOU CAN FLY...
...IS THE FIRST STEP TO LIFTOFF!
HAAH !!!
STAND BACK, NOW! A NEW LEGEND IS ABOUT TO UNFOLD!!!
1 2 3 4 5 ...
6 7 8 9 10 11 12 13 14 15 16 ...
INCREDIBLE!! HE'S SETTING ONE NEW RECORD AFTER ANOTHER AS WE SPEAK!!
NO WAY...
22 23 24 25 ...
....
32 33 34 35 36 37 38 ...
...?
BEEP
BEEP BEEP
Ku?
ANTI-GRAVITY MACHINE

125
126
127
128
AMAZING, MISTER SER-GEANT, SIR!
...HUH?
FLOAT
MISTER SER-GEANT ...SIR...?
M-MISTER SERGEANT?
FLOAT
FLOAT
FLOAT

WELL, WELL...I KNEW SOME-THING WAS GOING ON!
BEEP
BUT STILL... I WANT TO TRY!
I DID IT!!
TO BELIEVE YOU CAN FLY...
...IS THE FIRST STEP TO LIFT-OFF!
SHEESH. WHAT A BIG FAT LIAR.
....
WELL DONE!
AMAZING, NATCHI!

KERORO WANTED TO STOP, BUT HE COULDN'T ...
3285
3286
...
......
...AND AFTER A WHILE, HE JUST STOPPED COUNT-ING.
TO BE CONTINUED

THE NIGHTS GET LONGER...

...AND THE SCENT OF OSMANTHUS, ONCE AGAIN, FILLS THE AIR.

ENCOUNTER XCVIII
TRICK OR THREAT? A HALLOWEEN INVASION!

ENCOUNTER XCVIII
TRICK OR THREAT? A HALLOWEEN INVASION!

IT TAKES REAL COURAGE TO GET RID OF THE THINGS YOU COLLECT.
UNRAVEL
PERHAPS I SHOULD FOLLOW MASTER FUYUKI'S EXAMPLE AND...

Halt
NO...
...I WON'T.

OH...?
世界の怪物達の全てが解る
WHAT'S THIS?

LOOK, NATSUMI-CHAN! LOOK, LOOK!
THAT PUMPKIN HAS A FACE DRAWN ON IT.
HALLOWEEN
SALE
THAT'S A JACK-O-LANTERN, KOYUKI-CHAN. FOR HALLO-WEEN!
"HELLO IN" WHAT?
NO...IT'S A FESTIVAL THAT CAME FROM AMERICA... OR WAS IT FROM ENGLAND...?
ANYWAY, IT'S A HARVEST FESTIVAL... A CELTIC THING... FULL OF MONSTERS... SOMETHING LIKE THAT. RIGHT?
NATSUMI DIDN'T INHERIT THE SAME GENES FUYUKI DID.

WELL, IT'S CUTE, ANYWAY!
RIGHT! IT'S CUTE!
SAY! THERE'S GOING TO BE A HALLOWEEN PARTY IN THE PARK TOMORROW!
NPG
HALLOWEEN PARTY
10.31.MID NIGHT
WOULD YOU LIKE TO GO, KOYUKI-CHAN?
YES, YES!!
UMN
KERORO PLATOON SECRET UNDER-GROUND BASE
MONSTER!!
Mua haha ha ha!
IT'S THE AGE OF MONSTERS FROM NOW ON!!!
A MENACING EXISTENCE, FEARED BY ALL POKO-PENIANS!!
IF WE CAN JOIN FORCES WITH THESE "MONSTERS"... THOUGH OUR STRENGTHS WOULD DIFFER... WE WOULD BE ALL FOR ONE AND ONE FOR ALL!!
VRRRRMM
CORPORAL GIRORO!
WH-WHAT?
GO!
HUH?
GO FORTH... AND SEEK THEM OUT.
STOP BEING A FOOL! HOW CAN I SEEK OUT SOMETHING THAT MIGHT NOT EVEN EXIST?!!
HOW CAN YOU KNOW UNLESS YOU LOOK FOR THEM?!!

KULULU, BEGIN INVESTIGATION ON THIS MATTER IMMEDIATELY!
Ku ku ku... AYE, SIR.

I CAN JUST SEE MYSELF AS THE LEADER OF ALL MONSTERS! I MIGHT EVEN HAVE A PLACE IN SHOWBIZ!
OHH, I CAN'T WAIT! I'M GOING TO BE SO COOL!

KULU KULU
GEROGEROGER
GERO GERO
KULU
KULU

NISHIZAWA MANSION

YAY !!

KNOCK
KNOCK

OH! TAMAMA-SAMA!
HEE HEE HEE...
TRICK OR TREAT!

OH DEAR. I WILL GIVE YOU A TREAT... SO...NO TRICKS, PLEASE?
OKAY! NO TRICKS FOR YOU!

WAHOOOO!!

TRICK OR TREAT!
TRICK OR TREAT!

M-M-M-MOMOTCHI! LOOK HOW MUCH CANDY I GOT!!
OH! HOW NICE, TAMA-CHAN. ♪

I LOVE HALLO-WEEN!!
Help me...I'm sinking in my candy...!
WHEN I CONQUER POKOPEN, EVERY DAY WILL BE HALLO-WEEN!!

GRIN...

ALL RIGHT, THEN, TAMA-CHAN. STAY HOME TOMORROW LIKE WE PROMISED, OKAY? ♡
OH, YES! I WILL!!

PHEW ...
GOOD GOD.

GIRORO-DONO!
TMP
OH. IT'S YOU, DORORO.

POKO-PENIAN MON-STERS...?
WHAT DO YOU THINK? THINK THEY EXIST?

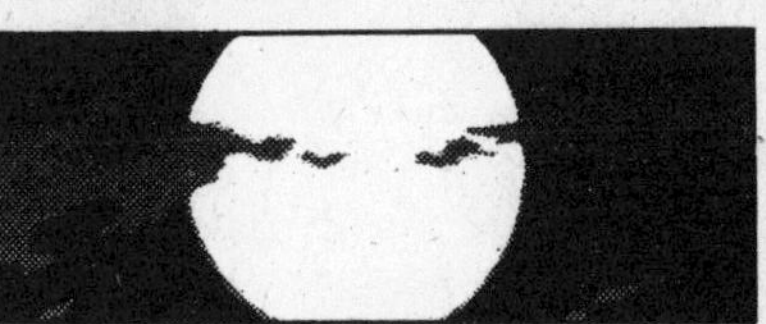

I MEAN, THEY DON'T...
...BUT WHAT IF THEY WERE HIDING EXPERTLY ENOUGH TO MAKE US THINK THAT THEY DID?

THEY WOULD BE FORMID-ABLE ENEMIES, INDEED...
...BUT ON THE OTHER HAND...

...WE, TOO, MIGHT BE MONSTERS BY POKOPENIAN STANDARDS.
HEH HEH... THAT'S TRUE.

FLAP
FLAP

OCTOBER 31

Chirp

Chirp

FUYUKI...
FUYU... FUYUKI...
WHOA! IT'S LATE!
I'M LATE FOR SCHOOL!!
GOODBYE!!
IF I HURRY ...
...MAYBE I'LL MAKE IT...!
huff
huff
Sniff
SCENT OF...
...OSMANTHUS.
SMIRK

H-HELLO...!
SMILE
FUYUKI!!
NA-TSUMI!
WHY DID YOU RUN OUT OF THE HOUSE?
YOU BETTER HURRY, TOO, OR YOU'LL BE LATE FOR SCHOOL!
...WHAT ARE YOU TALKING ABOUT?
?

IT'S ONLY 7:30!
HUH?!

はっ
?

A TRICK ...?

DING-DONG
キンコーン
A HALLOWEEN PARTY?
Y-YES. TONIGHT. OUR GROUP IS SPONSORING IT.
AND, UM... IF YOU'RE FREE... WOULD YOU LIKE TO JOIN ME?
YES, SIR! RIGHT ON!
S-SURE! SOUNDS LIKE FUN!

TONIGHT I'LL SAY "TRICK OR TREAT" TO FUYUKI-KUN...
...AND THEN GIVE HIM A TREAT (ME)!
Kyaaaa!!
YOU'LL DO IT MY WAY, RIGHT?
SHUT UP! THIS CALLS FOR ME!
I SHALL CALL IT, "OPERATION: TRICK OR ME"!!

THIS IS YOUR LAST NIGHT AS A BACHELOR, FUYUKI-KUN!
IT IS A HARVEST FESTIVAL, AFTER ALL!
Guehhh!
I FEEL A SUDDEN CHILL.
OH, WELL. IT IS FALL...

KERORO!!

GI-MEOW!
WHY THE HELL ARE WE DRESSED LIKE THIS?!!
Ooh, cute!

COMRADES! WE ARE BLESSED THIS DAY WITH HE CHANCE OF A LIFETIME!
A CHANCE THAT IS CALLED: HALLOWEEN PARTY!!
YES! WITH THESE FLIMSY DISGUISES, WE WILL JOIN THE PARTY...AND WITH NO ONE BEING THE WISER...
...WE'LL BE ABLE TO PERFORM INVASION CTIVITIES!!
Kuru kuru kuru!

SALLY FORTH, KERORO PLATOON!!!
TONIGHT, WE GIVE POKOPEN THE "TRICK OR TREATMENT"!!
Just a taste of the pain to come! ♪
UNFORTUNATELY, BECAUSE THEIR FACTS WERE HASTILY GATHERED, THE PLATOON IS SLIGHTLY MISINFORMED!

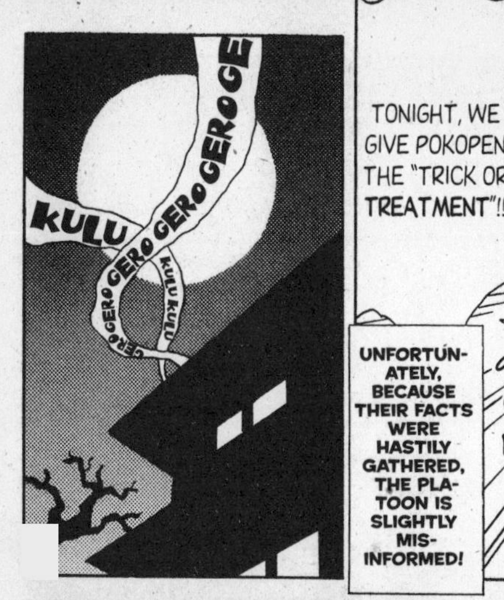
KULU
GEROGEROGEROGEROGE
KULUKULU

NEO-INOKASHIRA PARK HALLOWEEN BASH!!

WHAT A GREAT ATMOSPHERE!

PEOPLE FEAR THE DARK...
...BUT ARE STILL ATTRACTED TO IT. --623
... THERE.

EACH WITH THEIR OWN EXPEC-TATIONS ...

... HUMANS AND ALIENS GATHER AROUND THE JACK O' LANTERN ...

おおお
CLICK!
...AND THE PARTY OF DARKNESS BEGINS.
Welcome Halloween

THERE... THERE'S KERORO-KUN!
I SEE. SO... LEAVES HIDDEN AMONG LEAVES.

SOB... I'LL BET THEY'RE HAVING FUN.
I WONDER... IF THEY'LL LET ME JOIN THEM.

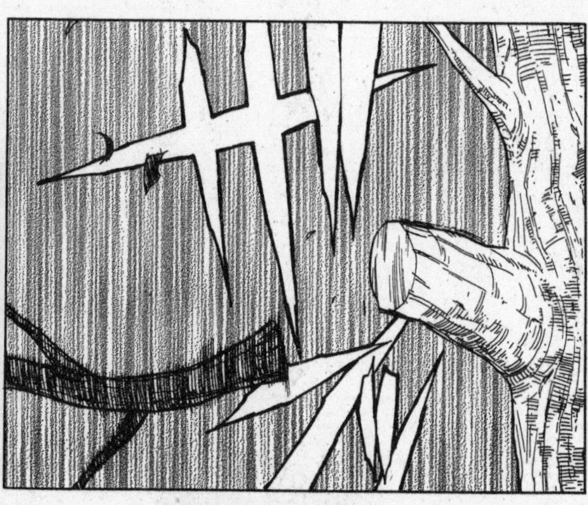

EH...?
WHO GOES THERE?!

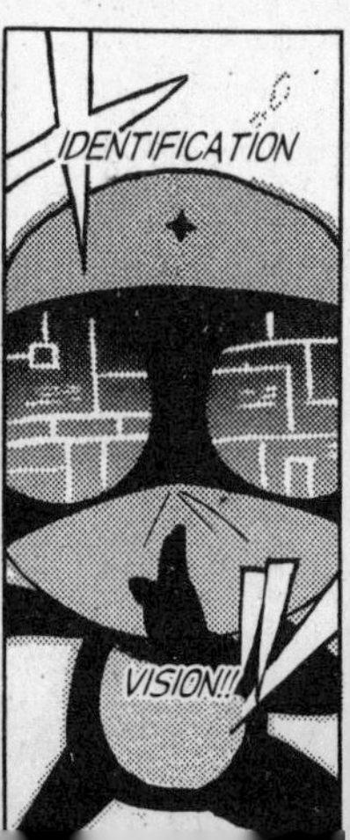
IDENTIFICATION
VISION!!

IDENTIFICATION... FAILED?!
UNIDENTIFIABLE
IMPOSSIBLE!!

HAAAAH!!
LEAPING SWORD TRICK SHIMEN-SOKA!
Shabah!

?!!
TMP

IT SAW THROUGH MY ASSASSIN ANTI-BARRIER...

...REPELLED MY ATTACKS EFFORT-LESSLY...

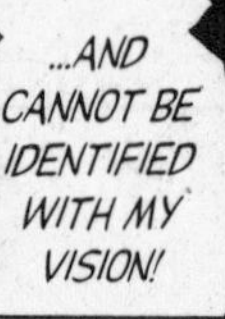
...AND CANNOT BE IDENTIFIED WITH MY VISION!

A FOR-MIDABLE ENEMY INDEED!
WHO COULD IT BE?!

ZING!
PEOPLE REALLY GET INTO THIS STUFF, EH, KOYUKI-CHAN?
UH, GOTTA GO! SORRY, NATSUMI-CHAN!
KOYUKI-CHAN?!
DORORO IS IN DANGER!!
COOL!
LOOK, A NINJA!
WELL, WELL... ISN'T THIS NICE?
WELL, MEN?! HOW DOES IT FEEL FIT IN SO WELL?!!
TO BE ABLE TO WALK ABOUT IN THE OPEN LIKE THIS IS A DREAM COME TRUE! ♪
IT'S LIKE A DREAM FOR ME, TOO...
...TO WALK SIDE BY SIDE WITH YOU, UNCLE!
SAY...WHAT SAY WE FORGET ABOUT TONIGHT'S SCHEME AND GO TO YODO-BASHI?
OOH...I HEARD THEY OPENED A HUGE ONE IN AKIHABARA.
WAIT, YOU IDIOTS!!!

SLITHER
Geroooo...!
KERORO ?!
UNCLE ?!

NO! AN ATTACK BY ENEMY ALIENS?!
THE HUNTERS ARE NOW THE HUNTED...!
NO TIME FOR JOKES, KULULU! LET'S MARCH!

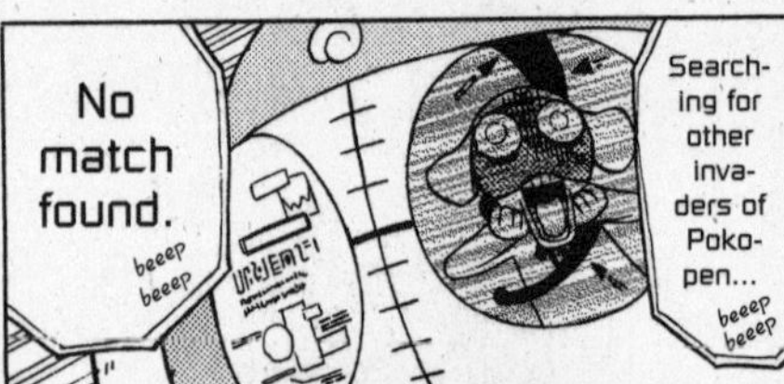
Searching for other invaders of Pokopen...
beeep beeep
No match found.
beeep beeep

Ku ku ku...
MAYBE...
THIS ONE'S "REAL"...

KERORO! WHERE ARE YOU?!

KA-SHUK
THERE!

!!
SLITHER
SLITHER

NOOO...
ARGH...!
KULULU!
I NEED BACKUP!!
SLITHER
SLIP

Ku ku ku ...
SORRY... NOT THE ATHLETIC TYPE...
SLITHER
SLITHER
SLITHER
WHAT ON EARTH...
...IS THIS...?!
SLITHER
SLITHER
SLITHER

LISA...
LISA...
...I'VE DONE MY PART.
NOW...DO YOURS.
...FUYUKI...
I WONDER IF THIS IS TOO BOLD... ♡
SO, WE'RE DOIN' THIS HALF AND HALF?!
"TRICK OR ME"...
...WHAT WILL FUYUKI-KUN WILL SAY TO THAT?
NISHIZAWA-SAN!
H-H-HE'S HERE!!

HINATA-KU--
?!

HUH...?
SCENT OF... ...OSMANTHUS...

LET'S GO...
...FUYUKI.
HUH?!

EH...
EH?!
HINATA-KUN?!
N-NISHIZAWA-SAN!!
HEY, HEY!
LOOK! THEY'RE FLYING!
WH-WHAT THE HELL WAS THAT?!!
CALLING HIM...
...BY HIS FIRST NAME... WITHOUT EVEN USING "-KUN"?!

HUT!
PAUL!!
SUPER ARMOR II FORTIFICATION IS COMPLETE, MY LADY!!
DEVELOPED BY NISHIZAWA GROUP "SUPER ARMOR II" (WORKING NAME) ENABLES AN EXPONENTIAL LEAP IN POWER BY ELIMINATING DEPENDENCY ON REAL NUMBERS. INCREASES TAMAMA CELL RENEWAL FACTOR BY 50%
YOU WON'T GET AWAY FROM ME!!

WHOA! THAT WAS ONE AMAZING SHOW!
NISHIZAWA GROUP REALLY PULLS OUT ALL THE STOPS!

BEEP
I never asked for your help, you know.
@Ⅲ@

WHAT DOES THAT MEAN?
!!

OH, IT'S THAT NINJA GIRL...
IS SHE OFF TO ANOTHER PARTY?

WAIT, YOU!!!
A... HUMAN ...?

!

VOOP!
HYAAAAAH!

ANOTHER ONE...

WHO ARE YOU?!
AND WHAT DID YOU DO TO DORORO?!

IS THIS THE PARTY?
CAN I JOIN YOU?

HEH HEH... ♪
JUST AS I THOUGHT.
THERE'S A LOT OF STRANGE ONES IN THIS TOWN...
EH...?
Hah

VOON
VOON

OUT OF MY WAY...
I'M TAKING FUYUKI.
TO BE CONTINUED

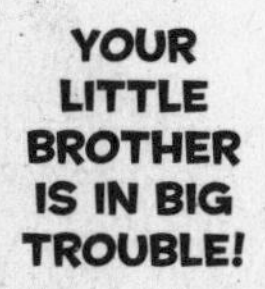

ENCOUNTER XCIX MESSENGERS FROM THE DARK: FUYUKI'S RESCUE!

ENCOUNTER XCIX
MESSENGERS FROM THE DARK: FUYUKI'S RESCUE!

WHEN YOU SAY YOU'RE TAKING HIM...
...WELL, I GUESS THAT COULD MEAN A NUMBER OF THINGS, BUT...

HOW DARE YOU?!!

HOW DARE YOU SPEAK TO HIM THAT WAY?!
I WON'T LET YOU TAKE HIM THAT EASILY!!!

MOMOKA IMPACT!!!
AND ON THAT EMOTIONAL NOTE...

HYEEE-EEH!

EH...?
FLASH
MOMOKA'S FEELINGS

MO-MOKA-CHAN!
I'M HERE TO HELP!!

LEAPING SWORD TRICK--
FLYING SNAKES !!

WAIT, EVERY-ONE!
YOU'RE FOR-GETTING ABOUT ME!
PA-CHINK!
EEEEP!
CLINK
SHE'S GOOD!
ONMYODO? NO...BUT VERY SIMILAR.
WHAT IS SHE?
CLINK CLINK
CLINK CLINK
CLINK CLINK

GLARE!!
Ack!

WELL... UH...
...I THINK I'LL JUST STAY OUT OF THIS ONE!

YOU EARTHLINGS ARE VERY STRANGE.
YOU ALMOST REMIND ME OF THE DARK RACE.
DARK...
...RACE?

BUT I'M TIRED OF ALL THE MEDDLING.
I SHALL DO WITH YOU AS I DID WITH THEM.
ZAWA
ZAWA ZAWA
CROIX DU SUD OMBRE... CROIX DU SUD FORCE...!

A...GORGON?!

EVERY-ONE, WATCH OUT!!
DON'T LOOK AT HER EYES!!

HUMANS ARE NOT OUR ENEMIES.

I KNOW.

TO OUR WORLD.
FUYUKI-KUN!!
MUTSUMI-SAN!

KINDA LIKE A SCARY BOOK I READ WHEN I WAS LITTLE.
......
BUT BEING LEFT BEHIND...
...HAS ITS OWN KIND OF FOREBODING.

WHAAAT?!
F-FUYUKI'S BEEN...
...KIDNAPPED?!!

KULULU, TOO...AND OTHERS, I THINK.
THEY ATTACKED US SUDDENLY...
WHO?! WHY?!

WE WERE HAVING SUCH A NICE TIME... AND NOW...
IT'S LIKE... THE HARDER YOU FALL?
I CAN PINPOINT FUYUKI'S LOCATION USING THE TRACKING E-MAIL KULULU SENT ME...
...BUT HOW WILL WE ACTUALLY SAVE THEM?
THOSE GUYS WERE CAUGHT, TOO?
HOW COULD THIS HAVE HAPPENED ...?

I WILL GO!! I'LL RESCUE UNCLE!!
I'LL DESTROY THE WHOLE PLANET IF I HAVE TO!!
NO, MOA-CHAN! PLEASE DON'T DO THAT!!
I JUST WONDER ...
...WHY FUYUKI ...?
Look
HUH?! NO ONE'S HERE?! NO CANDY EITHER?!
NO ONE TOLD ME ABOUT THIS PARTY!!
MOMOTCHI TRICKED ME!!
Look
TAMAMA?!
TAMA ...?

MY APOLOGIES FOR THE VIOLENCE, FUYUKI HINATA.

IT'S JUST BEEN OUR MODUS OPERANDI FOR SO LONG...

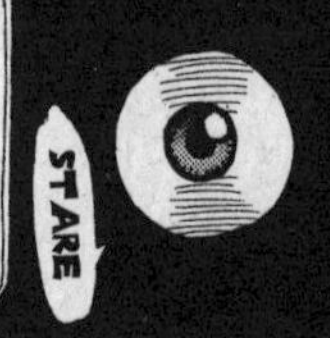

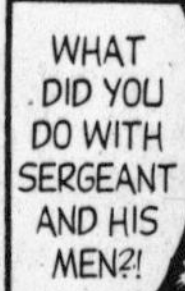

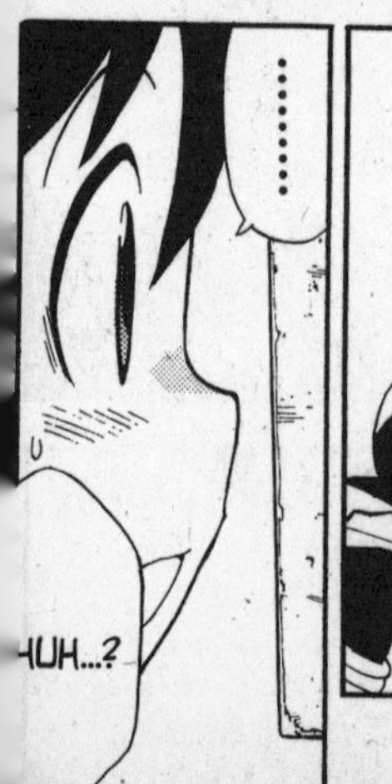

SER-GEANT?!
SOME-ONE! GET ME OUTTA HERE!
Ku ku ku
I AM DE-FEATED...
QUIET, YOU FOOL!!
HUNTING THOSE WHO HIDE IN DARK-NESS...
THAT IS OUR MIS-SION.
SLITHER

A GREAT NUMBER OF THE "DARK RACE" RESIDE IN THIS TOWN...
AND WE SOON DISCOVERED THAT YOU WERE AT THE CENTER OF IT ALL.
WHAT? BUT...
WELL... IT REALLY CAN'T BE DENIED.

WE FEEL YOU WOULD MAKE...
...AN EXCELLENT ALLY.

W-WAIT A MINUTE! THIS IS ALL HAPPENING SO QUICKLY!
THERE MUST BE SOMEONE ELSE WHO CAN HELP!
LIKE A MEDIUM, OR A FORTUNE-TELLER, OR...!
YOU KNOW! A PROFESSIONAL!

WHY ARE YOU SO FLUSTERED? YOU SMILED AT ME, DIDN'T YOU?
AT THAT MOMENT, WE ENTERED A COMPACT.

SMILE
SMILE
WHAT ...?
BUT... WHY ME...?

BE-CAUSE ...
...I LIKE YOU.

YOU ARE MINE NOW.
NO WAY!
SOME-THING ISN'T QUITE RIGHT HERE...
...BUT SINCE IT'S OUTSIDE OF OUR EXPER-TISE...
YOU SEEM TO BELIEVE THAT YOU HAVE FILLED THE WORLD WITH LIGHT, AND HAVE DARKNESS UNDER CONTROL ...
...BUT IN REALITY, YOU'VE ONLY CREATED A DEEPER, MORE SINISTER DARKNESS.
THIS IS WHY INCIDENCES OF INTRUDERS, SUCH AS THE ONES IN THIS JEWEL BOX, HAVE INCREASED...
Gero!

THE FURTHER YOU PUSH AWAY THE DARKNESS--CALLING IT "FAIRY TALES" OR "FOLKLORE" OR WHAT YOU WILL--THE BETTER IT IS FOR THE DARK RACE.
THE DARK DEPTHS OF THE OCEAN. THE HIDDEN DEPTHS OF THE FOREST. THE DEEPEST BOWELS OF THE EARTH.
THE WORLD AS YOU KNOW IT IS MUCH TOO SMALL.

THOSE WHO KNOW THE DARK ZONE KNOW THE ENTIRE UNIVERSE.
WELCOME TO OUR WORLD, FUYUKI HINATA!

BUT I...I DON'T WANT TO KNOW ALL THAT!!
I'M SATISFIED WITH MY KNOWL-EDGE FROM BOOKS!!
WHY DO YOU PUSH US AWAY?
DO YOU NOT LIKE ME?
TH-THAT'S NOT THE ISSUE.
I HAVE... MY OWN ISSUES ...
?!

KERORO PLATOON SPECIAL MOBILE ATTACK UNIT IS HERE!!!
ARE YOU ALL RIGHT, FUKKIE-SAN?!
BAM!
TMP
T-TAMAMA! MOA-CHAN!
LISTEN UP, VILLAIN-TYPES!! I, THE STRONGEST AND MIGHTIEST OF THE KERORO PLATOON...
...WILL RESCUE THE SERGEANT! AND THE OTHERS, TOO, WHILE I'M AT IT!!
AND I... SHALL HELP!
LIKE, ALL FOR ONE?
THE OTHERS' COMRADES...
HOW PESKY...
TAMAMA! THE SERGEANT AND HIS MEN ARE IN THAT BOX!
WATCH OUT! THEY WERE ALL DEFEATED!!

HEY...THIS IS A ONCE-IN-A-LIFE-TIME CHANCE TO SHOW OFF!!
THIS COULD BE MY CHANCE TO REDEEM MYSELF!
ONE GIANT LEAP FOR TAMAMA!!
UNCLE!!
THAT BRAZEN HUSSY! SHE'S STEALING MY LIMELIGHT!!
...
SLITHER
NO...UNCLE IS JUST A FEW INCHES AWAY...!
UNCLE... UNCLE...!
UNCLE!!!
HUH?!
Gero ?!
I JUST HEARD THE VOICE OF LADY MOA...!
LADY MOA! LADY MOA!
UNCLE!

UNCLE!
LADY MOA— HELP ME!
UNCLE!
LADY MOA!
UNCLE!
......
I DON'T HAVE ANY MORE TIME TO WASTE ON YOU EARTHLINGS.
I SHALL PUT YOU IN THE JEWEL BOX, ALONG WITH THEM.
Lady Moa...
DADDY!
!
JUST AS I THOUGHT...
I KNEW I SHOULDN'T HAVE COME HERE WITH THAT BROAD!
twitch
twitch
CURSES
HOW DARE YOU STEAL MY MISTER SERGEANT -- I MEAN--MY LIMELIGHT FROM ME!!
YOU SLIMY BITCH!
I'M JEALOUS! I'M JEALOUS! AND VERY ENVIOUS, TOO!
WHOA! NO, TAMAMA!!
NOT HERE...!

NO! YOU'LL DESTROY THE SERGEANT, TOO!!
SNAP
AAAAAAAH!
I DON'T GIVE A DAMN!!!
TSK...
RAISE
SAVE YOUR EFFORT LISA.
HUH?
IT'S NOT NEEDED.
JEALOUSY BALL

GEHHH?! IT DOESN'T AFFECT YOU?!
BUT...NO! HOW CAN THIS BE?!

IT SEEMS YOU BELONG TO THE DARK-NESS AS WELL...
...SO YOU HAVE NO POWER OVER ME.

WHA... ME...?
I'M... DARK?

T-TAMAMA!
TAMA?!
TAMA-CHAN?!

SHOOOMM

TA-MAMA!
HEY! NOW LOOK AT WHAT YOU'VE DONE!

GOOD HEAV-ENS...

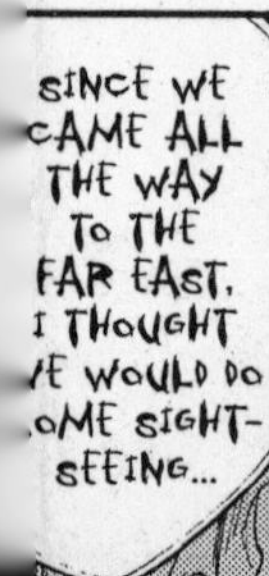
SINCE WE CAME ALL THE WAY TO THE FAR EAST, I THOUGHT WE WOULD DO SOME SIGHT-SEEING...

...BUT I'VE HAD ENOUGH TROUBLE FOR NOW.
LISA, WE WILL LEAVE IMMEDIATELY.
OUR NEXT DESTINATION IS ROMANIA.
ルーマニア!!
ROMANIA!!
LET'S GO, FUYUKI.
WAIT, WAIT! I DON'T WANT TO GO!!
DON'T BE A BABY.
PLEASE--WAIT A MOMENT!!
UNCLE'S DEAREST FRIENDS...
...AND UNCLE HIMSELF...I CAN'T LET YOU TAKE THEM!
DISGUISE: DEACTIVATED!
THE LORD OF TERROR
DESCENDS!!!
I SHALL RESCUE MY UNCLE!!

LORD OF TERROR? YOU'RE NOT... FROM THE DARK...?
URR...
URR...
DADDY?!
URRR... URRR.... URRRRRR ...
MOA-CHAN, DON'T USE YOUR FULL FORCE!
YOU AND TAMAMA ARE LIKE BIRDS OF A FEATHER!
NOT TO WORRY ...
...I'M ONLY MAKING A LITTLE SEA!
アジア海
The Asian sea.

WHAT IS THIS... SPRUNG FORTH FROM THE DEPTHS OF MY MEMORY?!
THIS IN-EXPLICABLE... DREADFUL... FEAR?!
?!!

SPACE
?
S--
ONE-TENTH!!!
APOCALYPSE
STOP, MOA-CHAN!!!
HALT

GWAAA AAH A!
GA GA GA GA GA GA GA GA GA
SOME-THING'S WRONG WITH HIM!
?!
D-DADDY ?!

SHAKE
SHAKE
Gerooo ?!
SERGEANT !!

KOYUKI-CHAN! MOMOKA-CHAN!
?
SHUUUU
Ku ku ku... I SEE ...
SO...HE WAS A "DARK NEBULAN" ...

DAD...
PSSSST
...DADDY...?
BEEP
AN...AN ALIEN?!

暗黒星雲
Dark nebula
A DARK AREA THAT EXISTS WHERE A PLANET COULD NOT QUITE BE FORMED... OR WHERE A PLANET ONCE EXISTED...
THIS ONE IS PROBABLY A RESIDENT... SOME KIND OF LIVING BODY.
ku ku ku ...
NO WONDER IT DIDN'T TURN UP IN MY SEARCH...

HE LOST HIS PLANET, CAME TO POKOPEN...
へえ～
...AND MUST HAVE GOTTEN WRAPPED UP THIS SO-CALLED "DARK ZONE."
KINDA SAD, REALLY.

YOU MEAN... WHERE A PLANET ONCE EXISTED...!
OH!
That is sad ...

?

I'M SORRY...I CAN'T BE ONE OF YOU...
...BUT IF YOU WANT, YOU CAN STAY AT MY HOUSE TONIGHT!

NO THANK YOU.
I'LL STAY HERE WITH DADDY.
WE'VE NEVER BEEN APART.

LAST NIGHT SURE WAS SOMETHING, EH, FUYUKI?

HA HA... YEAH. AND THERE I WAS, SO READY TO GIVE UP MONSTERS!
COULD'VE BEEN A WARNING FROM THE DARK ZONE!

YOU'RE SO POSITIVE, HINATA-KUN! ♡
IF I SEE THAT BROAD AGAIN, I'LL GET HER GOOD!!

!
Float
HUH?

SCENT OF...
OSMANTHUS.

YOU ?!

I DECIDED TO STAY IN THIS TOWN A WHILE LONGER.
SEE YOU AROUND, FUYUKI.
HEY...! YOU...! WAIT A MINUTE...!
WITH SOUTHERN-CROSS A NEW REGULAR ON THE SCENE, THE HINATA FAMILY NOW FACES WINDS FROM ALL QUARTERS.
TO BE CONTINUED

ENCOUNTER C
THE FROG WHO LOST NEW YEAR'S!

BEEP BEEP
Snore...
DECEMBER
31
TICK TICK
TICK TICK
TICK TICK
......
ぴくッ
URRR...
...GRRRMM...?
もぞ...
もぞ...
WHA... WHAT TIME IS IT?
INVADER: RESUR-RECTED!!

URRR...
ME ARMS FEEL LIKE SOME OTHER LAD'S!
(in heavy Irish accent)

OH...YES... I FELL ASLEEP SINCE THE DEATH MATCH OF NEW YEAR'S EVE...
slip
WHAT DAY IS IT?
AND... WHERE IS EVERY-BODY...?

Gero?!

PERIPHERAL INFORMATION: LACKING!! PHYSICAL ACTIVITY: RESTRICTED
IF THE SERGEANT WERE ATTACKED BY AN ENEMY NOW, IT WOULD BE OVER ALL TOO QUICKLY...WELL, DEPENDING ON HOW QUICKLY YOU READ.
WHAT SHALL I DO?!

I SHALL DO...THIS!!
PROBLEM: SOLVED!!

IF I TURN ON THE TV, I CAN FIND OUT!
OH--THE REMOTE!
roll roll roll roll roll
HALT

Everybody!! Happy New Year to you!!
NEW YEAR!
So... how was your New Year's?!
Melody Honey, had a great time, too! ♪
This year, we're broad-casting live for the first time! Let's have lots of fun, y'all!
EH ...?

It's January 5th, and it's nice and sunny! Now... Dooom!!!
PAPAPA HYARA HYARARI PAPAPA TERO TERO TERO
EH ...

RECORDED SHOWS HAVE ENDED...
...AND THE TV PERSONNEL ARE HIGH FROM HAVING HAD A LONG VACATION...
WHEN YOU LISTEN...
YOU CAN HEAR THE BUZZ AROUND TOWN...
Ah ha ha
Kyaa Kyaa
BRRRR
BANG BANG BANG
SO LET'S...
I SPENT NEW YEARS...
...IN MY SLEEP!!!
WA, HA HA HA!
AH HA HA HA!
THE STOCK PRICES ARE RISING...
GEONOGRAPHY IS IN THE LEAD!
BEPPU'S SUGINONI PALACE!

AH!

WHEN IT'S FINISHED, WE'LL GO SEE THE SUNRISE TOGETHER!
HMM? WHICH WAY WAS FRONT? YOU IDIOT! HA HA HA!

IN THE SPIRIT OF NEW YEAR, TAKE THIS, YOU USELESS POKOPENIAN... RYAAA!
INCRED-IBLE... MISTER SERGEANT, SIR.
EASY PEASY! AFTER WORK, WE'LL HAVE A SECOND NEW YEAR PARTY!
WHAT ABOUT A THIRD ONE?!
HA HA HA! WHY STOP THERE? WE'LL DO A FOURTH AND A FIFTH...!
WELL, PRIVATE TAMAMA--WHAT SAY WE GO FISHING?!
YEAH!
LEFTOVER TIME WILL BE DEVOT-ED TO MY HOBBY! ♪

WHAT FIFTH PARTY?!
I HAVEN'T DONE A THING.
IT'S NOT TOO LATE!!
YOU ARE TOO LATE.
KERORO PLATOON, ASSEMBLE!!
EVERYONE'S UTTERLY DISGUSTED, I'M SURE.
YES... KULULU...
SURELY HE WILL BE ABLE TO HELP!!

DO SOMETHING, SERGEANT MAJOR KULULU!!!

huff
huff

KULULU'S ROOM ALWAYS HAS BEEN LIT WITH SUSPICIOUS LIGHT, BUT...
KU-LULU?
KU LU LU ?!

しーん…
silence...

WHAT THE HECK'S GOING ON?!
WHERE ARE THE OTHERS?!

GIRORO?!

TAMAMA?!
I can't come to the phone right now.
Please leave a message at the tone.

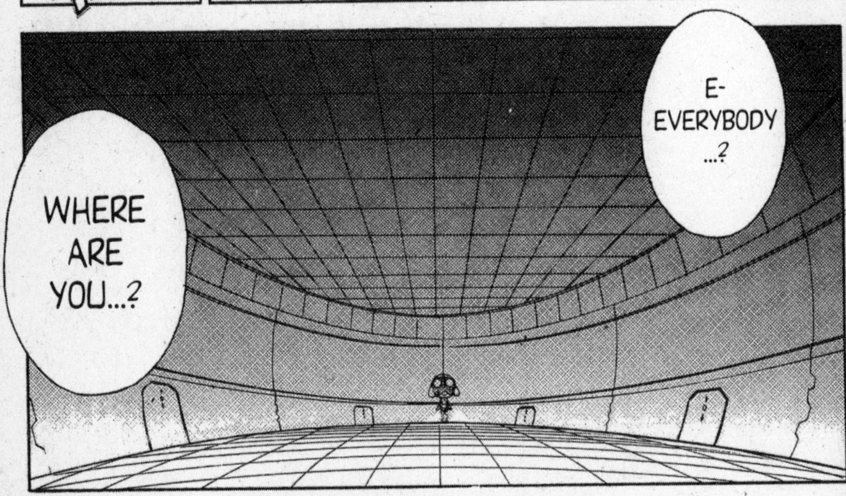

Note: He's flashing back to things that never happened.

MASTER FUYUKI!!
WINTER
MASTER NATSUMI?
GENERAL MOM?
AND--
ABILITIES OF THOUGHT AND JUDG-MENT IMPAIRED--
GENERAL MOM?!
MASTER FUYUKI?!
MASTER NATSUMI?!
FEELINGS OF DREAD AND LONLI-NESS ACCELER-ATED--
KACHA
W.C
FLUSHHH!!
HEH HEH...I SEE.
I AM BEGIN-NING TO UNDER-STAND.
THEY CAN'T FOOL ME.
IN MASTER NATSUMI'S ROOM, HER BELOVED MD PLAYER HAD BEEN CHANGED...
IN MASTER FUYUKI'S ROOM, I WITNESSED BOOKS THAT I'D NEVER SEEN BEFORE THROWN AROUND THE ROOM...
CLEARLY, SOMEONE HAS BEEN HERE!!

WHILE I WAS TAKING A LITTLE NAP...
I LET THE ENEMY MAKE ITS ATTACK!!
"WHILE I WAS SLEEPING..."
BY SERGEANT KERORO

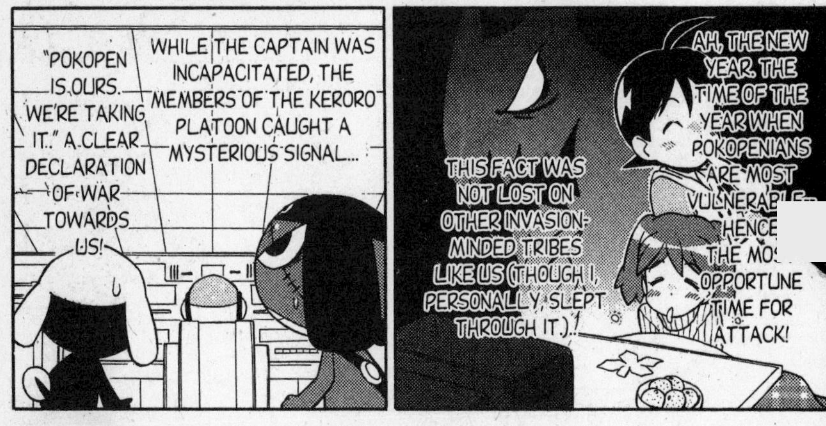
AH, THE NEW YEAR. THE TIME OF THE YEAR WHEN POKOPENIANS ARE MOST VULNERABL
HENCE THE MOS
OPPORTUNE TIME FOR ATTACK!
THIS FACT WAS NOT LOST ON OTHER INVASION-MINDED TRIBES LIKE US (THOUGH I, PERSONALLY, SLEPT THROUGH IT.).
WHILE THE CAPTAIN WAS INCAPACITATED, THE MEMBERS OF THE KERORO PLATOON CAUGHT A MYSTERIOUS SIGNAL...
"POKOPEN IS OURS. WE'RE TAKING IT." A CLEAR DECLARATION OF WAR TOWARDS US!

THIS IS AN EMERGENCY! WAKE UP KERORO NOW!
W-WAIT, GIRORO, SIR!!
WE CAN'T ALWAYS FALL BACK ON MISTER SERGEANT'S PROWESS!
THIS TIME WE MUST STAND...ON OUR OWN!!
YOU'RE ABSOLUTE-LY RIGHT, TAMAMA!
WE CAN DO IT, IF WE TRY!!
YEAH !!

Gueeeeh
WITHOUT ITS GALLANT COMMANDING OFFICER, KERORO PLATOON WAS UNABLE TO FUNCTION...AND ONE BY ONE, ITS MEMBERS WERE LOST.
BUT THEY WERE SAVAGELY DEFEATED!
GABOHEHE
KULULU!
AND THE POKOPENIANS THAT WERE LEFT BEHIND WERE...
WHY THIS ON NEW YEAR'S...?

I GUESS KERO-CHAN REALLY WAS HOLDING BACK THE BAD GUYS ALL THIS TIME.
I SHOULD HAVE GIVEN HIM MORE ALLOWANCE...

STUPID FROG...I MEAN, DEAREST SERGEANT KERORO!!
PLEASE FORGIVE MY PAST ACTIONS!!

DON'T WORRY, AS SOON AS HE WAKES UP...
POKOPEN WILL BE GIVEN BACK A NICE NEW YEAR!!

WE ARE FRIENDS.
I'VE FOUND YOU, POKO-PENIANS!!

DARN IT!!
ATSUMI!
MOM!!

SERGEANT!!!
RESPONDING TO THE DESPERATE CALL OF A DEAR FRIEND...
...THE LEGENDARY CAPTAIN, SERGEANT KERORO, AWOKE FROM HIS DEEP SLUMBER.

......
SO... THAT'S IT...

DOGGONE INVADERS!
WHY DON'T THEY TAKE NEW YEAR'S OFF FOR A CHANGE?!

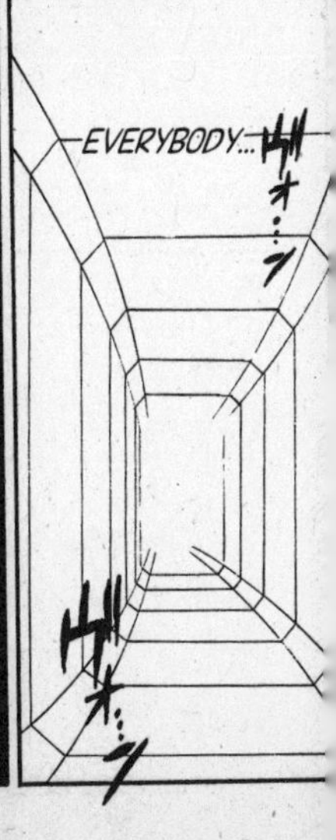
EVERYBODY...

MISTER SERGEANT SIR!
KERORO!

パーティー
本気
笑い

手動
THE HATCH IS OPEN, UNCLE. ♡
I SHALL...

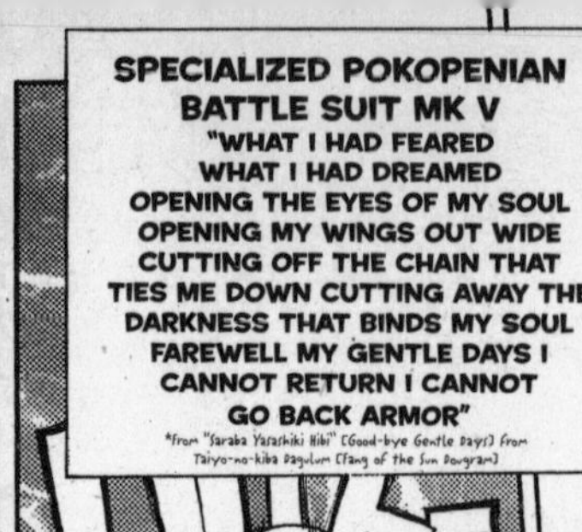
SPECIALIZED POKOPENIAN BATTLE SUIT MK V
"WHAT I HAD FEARED WHAT I HAD DREAMED OPENING THE EYES OF MY SOUL OPENING MY WINGS OUT WIDE CUTTING OFF THE CHAIN THAT TIES ME DOWN CUTTING AWAY THE DARKNESS THAT BINDS MY SOUL FAREWELL MY GENTLE DAYS I CANNOT RETURN I CANNOT GO BACK ARMOR"
*from "Saraba Yasashiki Hibi" [Good-bye Gentle Days] from Taiyo-no-kiba Dagulum [Fang of the Sun Dougram]

AVENGE EVERY SINGLE ONE OF THEM!!

GASHA
JAKON

I SHALL RECOVER...
THE TIME [NEW YEAR] THAT I HAD LOST!!

SERGEANT KERORO, SALLY FORTH!!!
WELL... I GUESS I'LL START.
GASHAN
AH...

GENTLE WIND...

IT'S SUNNY...
MAYBE I'LL START WORKING ON ZOK...

NO, NO, NO!
ガビーン ガビーン
REMEMBER, INVASION, INVASION!
...?
Mew?

*The New Year's shrine visit

REMIND ME TO GIVE GIFT MONEY TO KERO-CHAN, TOO. ♪
I wonder if he's awake by now.
WHAT?!
WHY DO YOU HAVE TO GIVE A GIFT TO AN ALIEN?
WELL, HE HELPED OUT A LOT WHEN WE WERE CLEANING FOR THE NEW YEAR, AND...
EH ...?

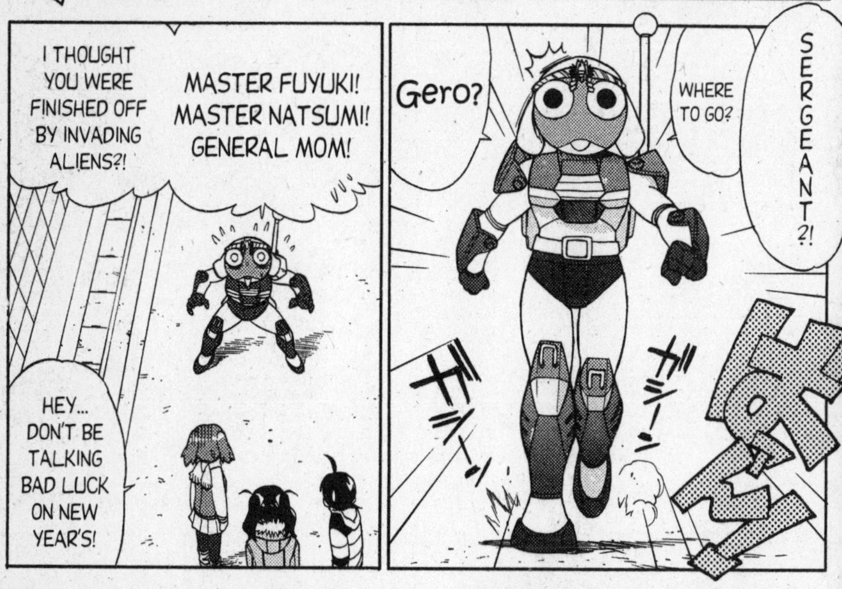
SERGEANT?!
WHERE TO GO?
Gero?
MASTER FUYUKI! MASTER NATSUMI! GENERAL MOM!
I THOUGHT YOU WERE FINISHED OFF BY INVADING ALIENS?!
HEY... DON'T BE TALKING BAD LUCK ON NEW YEAR'S!

THEN...THEN... WHERE DID YOU GO, LEAVING ME ALL ALONE IN THE HOUSE?!!
WE WENT TO A SHRINE!!
WE LEFT YOU BEHIND 'CAUSE YOU WERE ASLEEP.

I CALLED AND CALLED, BUT YOU WOULDN'T WAKE UP. SORRY, SERGEANT. I TRIED!
NOT TRUE!! WAKE ME HARDER NEXT TIME!!
ALL RIGHT, LET'S GO AGAIN! ONE MORE TIME! HATSU-MODE!
One more time!
Hatsu-mo-de!
UH, WEREN'T WE JUST THERE?
I WANNA LISTEN TO MUTSUMI'S PROGRAM!
BUT... WHAT ABOUT MY NEW YEAR?!
TOUGH. YOU SLEPT THROUGH IT.

I HAVE HAD IT!!!
(TO THE TUNE OF "AMAZON")
RELEASE OF THE TERRIFYING POWERS HIDDEN IN THIS SUIT SHALL REPLACE MY NEW YEAR'S GREETING TO YOU!!
W-WAIT A MINUTE! NOT HERE!!
SERGEANT'S FIRST "SNAP" OF THE YEAR!!
すぽっ

I'LL TAKE YOU.
LET'S GO TO HATSUMODE TOGETHER!
OH--AND I HAVEN'T GREETED YOU YET!
HAPPY NEW YEAR, SERGEANT!
HA--
HAPPY NEW YEAR!
BEST WISHES FOR THE COMING YEAR!

WE'RE OFF!
HAVE FUN!
IT'S A LITTLE LATE, BUT I'LL HAVE OZONI READY WHEN YOU GET BACK. ♡
YOU WON'T GET ANY IF YOU CAUSE TROUBLE!
CAN YOU MAKE SOME MOCHI, TOO?
OKAY!
SEE YOU LATER!

WE'RE NOT COMPLETELY IN TUNE WITH THE REST OF THE SOCIETY, BUT...
BY THE WAY...WHAT IS HATSU-MODE?
HMMM. WHERE TO BEGIN...?
THE HINATA FAMILY'S NEW YEAR IS JUST STARTING!

SAME TIME, IN OUTER SPACE.

TRAFFIC IS MOVING WELL ON ANDROMEDA BOULEVARD! THREE MORE POKOPEN HOURS, AND WE'LL BE THERE!
TRAFFIC IS LIGHT GOING THIS WAY DURING THIS TIME OF THE YEAR.
HOW WAS HOME, PRIVATE TAMAMA?
WELL, THEY ASKED ME IF I'D GAINED WEIGHT.
I WASN'T KEEN ON THE IDEA AT FIRST, BUT...
Did you lose weight?
You wanna switch?
Leave me alone!
ONE SHOULD HOME FOR NEW YEAR'S, AT LEAST...

I WONDER IF MISTER SERGEANT IS STILL SLEEPING...
BEEP BEEP
AH!!
GIRORO, SIR--LOOK, LOOK!!
A GIANT SPACE KING OCTOPUS. IT MUST BE AT LEAST 2,000 KILOMETERS LONG!!
HOOO... THAT'S GOOD LUCK.
PERHAPS THIS YEAR...
I, TOO... WILL AT LAST...
?

Large-scale anti-neutron reaction!
ENEMY ATTACK?!
WHAT THE... WHAT THE...?!
EVERYBODY IN KERORO PLATOON...
...HAPPY NEW YEAR TO YOU! ♡
I'M JUST COMING BACK FROM HOME, TOO.
HOPE YOU HAVE A VERY GOOD YEAR! ♡
THE GIRL FROM THE ANGOL TRIBE.
TSK... IS SHE BAD LUCK OR WHAT?
GET READY, TROOPS--THIS YEAR, WE'LL TAKE POKOPEN THIS YEAR FOR SURE!!
GOOOO US!!
LIKE, A DREAM COME TRUE?

ARE YOU READY ?
WHEN-EVER YOU ARE...
HAAH!

EH HEH HEH HEH HEH! ♪
Friends
-Koyuki Azumaya
IT'S A DRAW.
Best freinds!
-Dororo

BEST WISHES FOR THE NEW YEAR!
MASTER KOYUKI, YOUR PENMANSHIP IS TERRIBLE.
DORORO, YOU CAN'T SPELL.

*Very good luck **Very bad luck

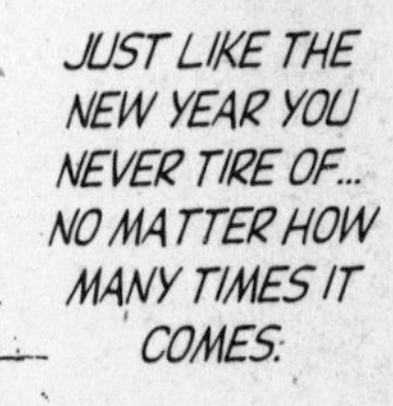

THE BEST TO YOU THIS YEAR, SERGEANT KERORO.

TO BE CONTINUED

BONUS ENCOUNTER ENCOUNTER C.5 THE DOOR OF TRUTH...

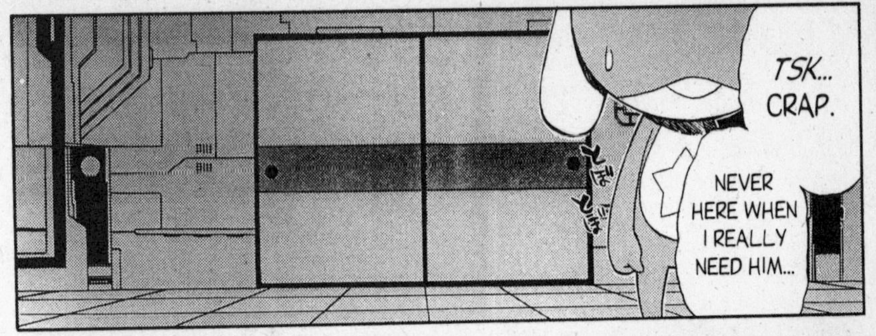

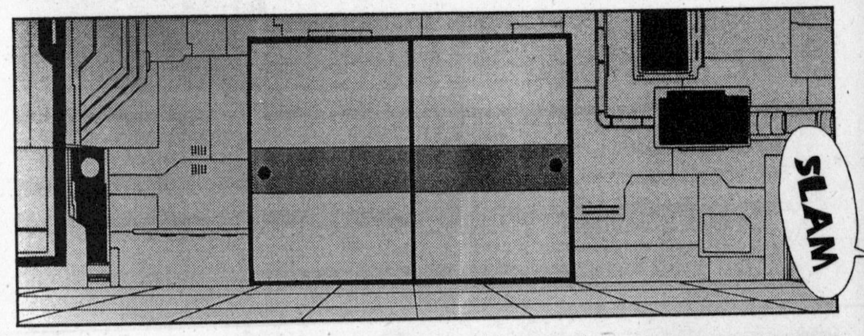

TO BE CONTINUED

GUEEEEEH!

JAPAN STAFF

CREATOR
MINE YOSHIZAKI

BACKGROUNDS
OYSTER

FINISHES
GOMOKU AKATSUKI
ROBIN TOKYO
TOMMI NARIHARA
634
EIJI SHIMOEDA

TO BE CONTINUED IN VOL 13

MUKURO-CHAN

THE INVASION CONTINUES!

HUMANITY'S DOWNFALL IS IMMINENT!

GERO! GERO! GERO!

GREETINGS, POKOPENIANS! HAVE YOU MISSED ANY EXCITING DETAILS SURROUNDING YOUR EVENTUAL SUBJUGATION? FEAR NOT. VOLUMES 1 THROUGH 11 OF *SGT. FROG* WILL BRIEF YOU. AND READING ABOUT ALL OF MY FAILED PLOTS AND SCHEMES WILL ONLY LULL YOU INOT A FALSE SENSE OF SECURITY!

TOKYOPOP MANGA SUPPLEMENT

WWW.TOKYOPOP.COM

I LUV HALLOWEEN VOL. 3

FH FAIRVIEW:HOSPITAL

X-RAY REPORT : NOTES

IT'S LIKE TAKING CANDY FROM A DEAD GUY...

They say bad things come in threes, and the third round of trick o' treating is here amidst a close encounter of the disturbing kind.

"I Luv Halloween is pure filth."
- Robert Sparling, fanboyplanet.com

"Crass, tasteless, and brilliant."
- Newtype USA

FOR MORE INFORMATION VISIT:

STOP!

This is the back of the book.
You wouldn't want to spoil a great ending!

This book is printed "manga-style," in the authentic Japanese right-to-left format. Since none of the artwork has been flipped or altered, readers get to experience the story just as the creator intended. You've been asking for it, so TOKYOPOP® delivered: authentic, hot-off-the-press, and far more fun!

DIRECTIONS

If this is your first time reading manga-style, here's a quick guide to help you understand how it works.

It's easy... just start in the top right panel and follow the numbers. Have fun, and look for more 100% authentic manga from TOKYOPOP®!